stay with me

stay with me

BY GARRET
FREYMANN-WEYR

HOUGHTON MIFFLIN COMPANY
BOSTON 2006

WWW.HOUGHTONMIFFLINBOOKS.COM

THE TEXT OF THIS BOOK IS SET IN VENETIAN.

LIBRARY OF CONGRESS CATALOGING-IN-PUBLICATION DATA

FREYMANN-WEYR, GARRET, 1965–
STAY WITH ME / BY GARRET FREYMANN-WEYR.
P. CM.
SUMMARY: WHEN HER SISTER KILLS HERSELF, SIXTEEN-YEAR-OLD LEILA GOES
LOOKING FOR A REASON AND, INSTEAD, DISCOVERS GREAT LOVE, HER
FAMILY'S TRUE HISTORY, AND WHAT HER OWN PLACE IN IT IS.
ISBN 0-618-60571-1 (HARDCOVER)
[1. SISTERS—FICTION. 2. SUICIDE—FICTION. 3. INTERPERSONAL RELATIONS
—FICTION. 4. NEW YORK (N.Y.)—FICTION.]   I. TITLE.
PZ7.W5395ST 2006
[FIC]—DC22

2005010754
ISBN-13: 978-0618-60571-2

MANUFACTURED IN THE UNITED STATES OF AMERICA
VB 10 9 8 7 6 5 4 3

BUT YOU ARE, YOU KNOW, YOU WERE, THE NEAREST
THING TO A REAL STORY TO HAPPEN IN MY LIFE.

Renata Adler

For Tara and Teddie,
my first great loves

One

I DON'T THINK THIS IS WHERE ANYONE ELSE WOULD BEGIN, BUT IT'S THE EXACT RIGHT PLACE FOR ME.

Before she died, I used to spend time with my father's first wife. We had tea and very thin slices of gingerbread at her apartment on the West Side. Janie, as she insisted I call her, was often away for work (she worked right up until the end, right through chemo, right until she couldn't leave the hospital), and so we had no set time for our meetings. But we had an understanding that when she was in town, she would call me and I would come over.

I suppose it was an unusual arrangement, but I think its unusualness was the very thing that made it appealing to her. For me the visits were important

1

because I hoped Janie would help me to know my two older sisters somewhat better than I did. After all, my own mother had taught me valuable things—carpentry, cleaning up a bloody nose, how to change a tire on the side of a highway. If you knew my mother, you would kind of know me.

I'm not sure Janie taught me what she had taught my sisters, but I did learn little things about them from her. For example, Rebecca rarely returned phone calls, but Clare would stay late at the office until she had read every fax, returned every call, and made a to-do list for the next day. Rebecca liked any and all ice cream but Clare almost never ate dessert.

"And when she does, she does not eat it out of the carton," Janie said during one visit when she'd been too busy to buy cake. Which was why we were eating a half-empty pint of coffee chip with two spoons. Something Rebecca might do, apparently, but never Clare.

Sometimes Janie told me things that had nothing to do with my sisters. Things which sounded useful without my being sure they were. When I asked her about the first date she and Da had, Janie told me that she and Da had been introduced by one of those men whom *everyone* knew. They were at a cocktail party and Julian (Da's real name) asked if she'd allow him to buy her dinner.

Yes, she said, she would.

At the restaurant, he told her he knew she probably wouldn't order the cheapest thing on the menu for fear of offending him. However, since it was clearly the only good thing on the menu (Janie said it was a cheese and egg dish), he was going to order it and hoped she would too.

"I knew in that moment that I had been right to leave the party with him," Janie told me.

I loved everything about this story. That she was probably dressed up, that he asked permission to buy her dinner and that they both knew a man known by *everyone*. The way Janie had said *everyone* made me think that it meant something else entirely. What I didn't understand was how she could offend Julian by ordering something cheap.

"You never order the cheapest item while on a date," Janie said. "It might make him think you're worried he can't afford to buy you dinner."

It seemed to me that he would notice the price only if he *couldn't* afford to buy you dinner. In any event, my mother had always told me that when I started dating I should split the check so that I would never feel obligated to a man. Or to a boy. Or, as she was careful to put it, to *whomever*. Mom believes that it's best to be open-minded until you have all the facts. Then you can form a judgment. As I immediately did upon hearing Janie's explanation.

"You can't order the cheapest thing on a date?" I asked her, laughing. "That's ridiculous."

"I suppose it is," Janie said. "But you just don't do it."

I felt my sisters had gone out into the world equipped with information I had no idea how to use. Their lives seemed so far removed from mine and I wondered if I could close this gap by absorbing everything Janie said.

I always meant to ask Da who had taught him this ordering rule that I now knew. Only I didn't want to tell him I had been asking Janie about their first date. I didn't really want to remind him that I saw her. Our visits had begun four years ago, when I was twelve and my seventh grade English teacher had decided I was not *slow* or *lazy* or *unmotivated*. I was not even *stupid*. The right word, it turned out, was *dyslexic*.

4

This means, among other things, that I see letters backwards as easily as forward. That I stand on street corners incapable of telling left from right. That I worry beyond reason over the proper order of things. Over beginnings and ends. I read really slowly and often can't figure out what I've read.

Tell me something and I'll remember it, repeat it, and even write it down, although the spelling might be questionable. *Wednesday* always gives me pause (what's the first *d* there for?). Also any *-ough* words: *enough, though, throughout,* and forget the whole *i* before *e* rule. If I knew when they were pronounced *ay* as in *neighbor* or *weigh,* I wouldn't have a problem in the first place.

Clare and Rebecca also had dyslexia, but theirs was somewhat less crippling than mine. When Janie and Julian were still married, he decided that the girls' learning disorders were inherited from Janie.

"I should be grateful he was willing to blame the eating disorders on society," she said.

Clare was anorexic in high school and Rebecca threw up all through college. I'm not impossibly thin like Clare, but I'm thin enough and have the advantage of both liking food and eating it.

News of my dyslexia traveled through *the girls*, as

Da and Janie called them, to their mother. As I was now evidence that the dyslexia wasn't her fault, Janie told Rebecca that she owed me a good turn. Was there anything, in particular, Janie wanted to know, that I might want? A sweater, maybe? Perfume? Earrings?

"I'd like to meet your mother," I said to Rebecca, who was the only person to whom I'd ever be able to admit this.

Of the girls, Rebecca was my favorite because her interest in me was, while sporadic, believable. Clare, with an elegant kindness I was sure she'd learned from Janie, let me know that she would prefer a certain distance between us. *Nothing personal, understand,* she seemed to say, *it's simply easier this way.* I understood.

In a way, I was even grateful, because Clare's coolness allowed me to focus on Rebecca. My oldest sister's reputation as the family screwup and lost, secretive soul turned her tiny frame into a figure of importance and authority.

"You want to meet Janie? Wouldn't you like a real present?" she asked me, thinking I was going to hold out for theater tickets. Or a new sweater.

Rebecca was thirty-four at the time, getting divorced, and barely talking to her parents.

"Are you sure?" she asked.

"Yes," I said, surprised that this was not more obvious to everyone.

After all, my father's great love was not with my mother but with theirs. Janie and Julian's marriage didn't just produce my sisters, but a great ruin. *When I found him, he was ruined,* is exactly how my mother puts it. She means that he missed my sisters and was distracted by being lonely and confused. But I think something else was going on.

Da had apparently spent the three years between Janie's leaving and his meeting Mom by working all the time and going to the opera at night. Or staying home on the weekends he didn't have Clare and Rebecca with him and listening to big, sad music. He still has the albums even though we don't have a record player. They're all by Mahler or have the word *requiem* in them.

It's heartbreak music. The kind of heartbreak you get when you love someone who no longer loves you. It's not only the records that make me think love ruined him. Da has, in his study, a shelf of photographs from his life with Janie. They're mostly of the girls, but there's one with Janie in it that's my favorite.

Julian and Janie are standing in front of the ocean with Clare between them. Janie is wearing her sunglasses like a headband and Clare has a paper party hat on. Julian's hand is on Janie's shoulder and they're looking down at Clare, but also at each other. Something in my father's expression—a kind of drunken bliss—tells you: here was a great love. A love that was big, sweeping, and, in the end, impossible. But no matter the end, it was here. Right between them.

Da still got very quiet whenever Janie's name came up and he always put off calling her back when they had to talk about my sisters (a new boyfriend, a job, a medical thing or an apartment). I know he loves my mother. You can hear it in the way he calls her name—letting the *l* roll slowly into the *s* of Elsa. But I thought he could love Mom while also still having his great love be Janie. Of course, maybe I was wrong and that great love had vanished the minute they split up.

Since I had not been there to see or hear it for myself, I felt free to make up certain things. One way or another, I wanted to know the story of *before.* Then I might feel like less of a stranger when my sisters and my father were together.

"We aren't strangers," my mother would say. "It's

that they were a part of him first. It's not better, it's just first."

I knew she was right and Da was still with us, while his life with Janie was gone. But it had existed, and in a way, I came from it as much as Clare and Rebecca did. I looked at old photos, at my sisters, and on occasion at Da himself, and easily imagined what had held them and Janie together. Before it flung them apart.

A great love and a great ruin.

The very best information I had about Janie and Julian came from Rebecca, who had told me how Da spent the years between his marriages. The great love photograph itself was one Rebecca took on her twelfth birthday. The camera was a present from her parents and the frosting on her cake was, she said, full of sand. When I told Rebecca that yes, I wanted to meet her mother, I must have thought Janie could help me take stories which didn't belong to me and make them mine.

There were two important stories that Rebecca could not—or would not—help me with. The first concerned two hotels my father's family had owned since the early 1900s. They were lost long before my sisters were born. The hotel in Spain was sold to pay the debts of a gambling cousin. The bigger one in Egypt, where Da grew up, had to be sold when life there for Jews became impossible. The hotel in Alexandria has become a government building, but the one in Barcelona is still open for guests.

As far as Abranel family history goes, the story of the lost hotels belongs to Clare. She has the only photographs of them and she's the lawyer for a man who owns lots of hotels. She treats hotels like living, breathing things. The happiest I've ever seen her was talking about a contract that would deliver heated towel racks to hotels in Germany. If I told her I loved the lost hotels, that I had plans to visit them one day, she would be offended. They are hers to long for.

The other story Rebecca wouldn't speak of concerned the wide scars on the insides of her arms, which ran down toward her hands. She'd cut open her wrists two years before I was born and though I knew certain external details of *the incident,* which is how Da and Clare described it, I didn't know why she did it. Mother said that she doubted Rebecca herself knew, but I was sure there was a reason. An unwritten, secret story that Rebecca was waiting to tell me.

I certainly didn't think Janie would tell me about *the incident,* and I knew that the hotels were lost before she ever met my father. But I was anxious to check reality against my imagination. Against a birthday photograph from twenty-plus years ago. I never really knew why Janie agreed to meet me and my parents had no reason to object. It was easily arranged.

One meeting might have been enough for both of us, but since Janie was a lighting designer and I had recently figured out that plays were made for dyslexics, we developed other reasons for talk and tea and sweets. Plays have a structure built into them that helps me to keep events and characters straight. So it's easy to keep track of the order. Janie knew a lot about plays and I had a lot of questions. I had joined the drama department's tech crew at school, but it wasn't enough to build the sets. I wanted my ideas to be the ones that got built.

My mother could and did help me with the actual set building. From her I learned how to work with a blueprint. How to calculate weight and support. To shop for supplies and to let my hands lead me through the process. But Mom could not read a play and see the set.

Janie could do that. She could immediately see how to close the gap between a great idea and the impossibility of building it. Conversations with Janie were full of *How about just a hint of that?* or *Have you thought of working around this?* or *Lighting will fix it.* I often brought my ideas to Janie and she was the one who taught me never to start designing sets for the entire play.

"Find a scene," she said. "Or better yet, a corner of a scene. One person's single action. What are they doing and where are they doing it? Build your set on a tiny moment."

"Just one?" I asked her. "How do you know which to pick?"

"You start with a detail that most grabs your attention and move out," Janie said. "Don't impose your big idea on the play. For—"

"For the play itself is the big idea," I said, finishing for her.

Janie and Da both spoke in absolutes which were easy to remember but required, Rebecca said, more doubt than faith. The girls found my attachment to their mother hilariously peculiar and were forever trying to dilute it just a little. From Rebecca I found out that Janie had greeted the news of my mother's pregnancy by saying, *Julian's back-up plan.* And Clare told me that her mother had remarked that my name, Leila (from the Persian meaning "dark as night"), was *pretentious but serviceable.*

I thought Janie's comments were interesting. Up until I heard them, I had worried that I was the one daughter for whom Julian had not planned. Perhaps I was a back-up to my sisters, but since the girls didn't always like Da so much, maybe expanding his plan was smart. And the only thing I had ever had to say about my name was the rather lame *I am not a rock song* to people who called me Lay-la instead of Lee-la. Besides, as far as I was concerned, after all the time she'd spent talking to me about her work, Janie could pretty much say what she wanted. Clearly my sisters, into their thirties by the time I was ten, had forgotten just how precious attention is from a grownup who is not your parent.

I asked Janie about leaving my father only once.

"You look happy in the pictures," I said. "What happened?"

She was quiet for so long that I thought she was coming up with a polite way to tell me I was being rude. Instead she went to a cabinet in her bookshelves, opened it and poured herself a brandy. She did not add ice. Or water.

"How does it go? 'Things fall apart,'" she said, once

she had sat back down. "Wait, no. Throwing poetry at you is exactly what Julian would do."

Da does quote poetry rather a lot. I don't mind because, in poems, the meaning doesn't come from the order. And everyone gets confused reading poetry. Not just people like me.

"When things end, what matters is not that everything's in pieces," Janie finally said. "It's how you decide to carry them."

I thought that as nonanswers go, this one was pretty cool because she was miles away from saying that when love died, you picked yourself up and made the best of things. That you carried ruin with you was surely something I already knew from watching my father, but it seemed more believable spelled out by Janie.

It took a while, but I did find the poem. The one that she wouldn't quote. *Things fall apart.* It's not about divorce or great love; more a certain kind of violence. It's the first thing I think about when the city is attacked. And when Rebecca succeeds in killing herself. Pills this time. No scars, but no surviving either.

My sister's departure should be where to start. A more clever girl would open with it. But I, of course, go hopelessly backwards to Janie, dead a year by the time it happens. And then ahead until I can clearly see the decisions my father and Clare are making about their portion of ruin. I arrived when Rebecca's life was more than half over, and my share of what she leaves behind is therefore small. Just big enough to carry.

Two

IT'S A FEW DAYS AFTER THANKSGIVING IN THAT YEAR
WHICH IS ALREADY FULL TO BURSTING WITH BAD NEWS.
PARTICULARLY IF, AS WE DO, YOU LIVE IN THE CITY.

Da stays home from his hospital office every other
Tuesday to do paperwork. On those days, I let him
know I'm back from school and then leave him alone.
It's understood that nothing is to disturb him.

When the doorbell rings, I run for it, ready to sign
for a package. We don't do Christmas or Chanukah (*Secular means secular*, Da says), and Mom tries to make up
for it by giving me things I "need" during the last
month of every year. Of course, she has no time to shop,
so I get a lot of my not-presents from catalogues.

Only it's not a package. It's Raphael. Raphael
Barclay, who's sort of our cousin but not really.

Raphael's mother is my Aunt Ingrid, who's not really my aunt. She was once married to my father's brother, but he died—he drowned in the ocean—back when Da was still in Alexandria. A few years later, Aunt Ingrid married Raphael's father when the Abranel family was in Paris. That's where they first lived after leaving Egypt.

Keeping as little as that straight is almost impossible. And there's more.

While everyone was still in Paris, Raphael's father, who was American, introduced Janie, who was British, to Julian, who eventually became my father. The cocktail party where Janie and Julian met was in Paris. Raphael's father wasn't just an American who married Aunt Ingrid. Uncle Harold was, as Janie had described him to me, the man *whom everyone knew.*

Even if I often can't follow how, I know the Barclay family is a part of my family. That it's confusing is part of the proof that we all fit. Apparently, visual aids do help.

Rebecca told me that when Raphael dated Clare, he had to draw her a chart to prove they weren't related. Raphael is a lot like the hotels, in that he totally belongs to Clare. Even though they went out for less than three months and broke up when I was four. Janie told me that she thought Raphael was completely unsuited to

Clare, but she said that about everyone Clare dated.

I like Raphael. Everyone likes him. Janie had said if he would stop being in love with Clare, she would like him too. Mom felt that he'd be perfect for Clare. Something which amazed me, as she normally goes out of her way to avoid contradicting Janie's thoughts about my sisters. Raphael's a lab science person like my mother (she's a pathologist and he studies genetics), but he's a much better dresser than she is.

"Leila," he says.

"Hi," I say, and then, because I have only ever seen him here when it's Clare's birthday, "Clare's in Hungary."

She's either working there or visiting the superstar of her unsuitable boyfriends, whom *no one* likes. I do, though, because he's unbelievably beautiful and speaks with a great accent. More to the point, he lives in Budapest, which is where Clare's boss owns two apartment buildings. They're being renovated and she goes to Hungary a lot for work as well as unsuitable-boyfriend stuff, and as I am trying to remember what this particular trip is for, Raphael says,

"It's Rebecca. She's —"

At which point he covers his face with his hands and starts to cry, so I know nothing good is to follow and yet all I can think is that the only other man I've seen cry is my father when Janie died. It doesn't look that different on Raphael.

"Rebecca's killed herself," he says, and his voice breaks up, but the crying stops. "I'm sorry. Julian's office said he was here."

"He's working," I say, wondering if *killed herself* means something different from what I think.

Because, of course, Rebecca cannot have done this. There is simply no way on earth she did this. Even I know Janie will kill her. And then I remember.

"You'd better come in," I say, when what I mean is *Go away.*

Janie died last year, and until then no one ever noticed how old my father is. Now people ask all the time if he's my grandfather. This will more than finish his accelerated aging process.

"Oh, God," Raphael says, sliding his hands up under his glasses. "The cleaning lady called me. I'm the emergency contact when they're out of town."

After Janie died, Clare and Rebecca moved into their mother's rent-controlled apartment, and one of the many decisions that move involved was hiring a cleaning lady. My sisters are each messy, but in different ways (Clare with paperwork, Rebecca with clothes), and neither wanted to straighten up after the other. The cleaning lady is from Chile and incredibly cheerful. What English she has, she tends to sing; to me, for example, *Good morning, little one.*

For a split second I think that the truly unforgivable thing is that Rebecca let this woman, whose name I knew just two minutes ago, find her. And then I think entirely too much about what I do know of Rebecca's scars. Of *the incident.* Clare found her. Up at Janie's weekend house in Connecticut. In the tub and half dead. Blood everywhere.

Clare's in Hungary. Safe with her boyfriend. Good for Rebecca.

"I'll get my father," I say.

"Let me," Raphael says, handing me his coat, scarf, and briefcase.

Later, I will be grateful he gave me something to do. But right then, I am furious. Thank you, I am *not* the coat check girl. I think how stupid Raphael is, how useless, how a better person would have called my mother first and made sure she was here when Da got the news.

But Raphael didn't call her, which is how I know the news is true; Rebecca has killed herself. She always referred to Raphael as *our favorite cousin,* and I doubt he'll be thinking clearly for weeks. We're incredibly lucky he didn't tell Da over the phone.

So this is what being lucky means now.

When my mother comes home, summoned by a belated phone call, she finds me in the hall, sitting in front of the coat closet. I'm not crying—that won't come for months—but my body's too heavy for standing. Mother dumps her coat and bag on the floor.

"Oh, God, Leila," she says, crouching down to hug me.

Her arms hold harder than is comfortable, but I let myself match it until I can feel her relax.

"He'll never get over this," she says, standing up and sliding off her shoes.

And because my mother is capable and clever and more than equipped to handle crisis, I hear everything else she means.

Oh, God, Leila, I am so sorry.

Oh, God, Leila, how could she have done this.

Oh, God, Leila, we will do everything wrong.

Forgive me.

That we will do everything wrong seems unavoidable, no matter how competent my mother is. What could be more wrong than killing yourself? *How could she?* is the right question. And yet, poor Rebecca.

"I know," I say, thinking how Da will now be forever different. "But he might."

Mom disappears into the small room in which the girls slept on the rare occasions when they stayed over. The room where my father's real life is kept. Medical journals, mail, file folders, old records, and an entire shelf of photographs devoted to documenting a life that has now ended more than once.

Da wants Clare. It's all he wants.

"Where's Clare?" he keeps saying. He has to go with Raphael to the girls' apartment to meet the police and the medical examiner. I'd like to go with them, but explaining this, asking for it, seems so beside the point.

Raphael has offered to fly over to tell Clare in person. He doesn't think she should get the news on the phone. Raphael's father was really rich and he left a lot of money, so flying to Europe at the last minute is the kind of thing Raphael can afford to do. No one has ever told me what Uncle Harold did. I asked Janie once and she said, "Harold? The man printed money." I've never had the chance to find out what *printed money* really means.

"Clare's coming home in two days," my mother says.

"I think we can give her a day of peace."

"No," Raphael says. "She'll never forgive us. A day is too long not to know."

"If you fly, it will be tomorrow before you reach her," Da says. "I've got to call her."

I remember how it was Clare who called Da when Janie died. His nose started to bleed before he even got off the phone. As I went to wrap ice in a towel, I felt so badly for my sister. I knew that if I were Clare right then, I'd want someone to take care of me. If you have a fever or just a case of the blahs, my father is great. He's the first one there with aspirin, clear liquids, or tickets to an extra-fun musical.

But if your news is bad enough to upset him too (*I got another C in English, Da*), forget it. I remember giving Da his ice pack as I made a quick list of where the blood needed to be cleaned from—his wrist, his tie, and the cover of his checkbook. I hoped that Janie had died peacefully in her sleep. And that my sisters would know how to do whatever Da could not.

I don't hear the call when my father reaches Clare. I assume he tells her she can come stay with us for a while and that she says no. I hope her boyfriend does for Clare whatever Rebecca did for her when Janie died.

Although it seems more likely that there's nothing one can do this time. While it's easy to tell that my sisters weren't close in a *let's stay up and talk* kind of way, they were each what the other one had. Or so it seems to me. Seemed to me.

We will not just do everything wrong. We will need entirely new verbs.

Three

AFTER DA AND RAPHAEL HAVE LEFT, I call Ben. All I say is my sister's name and the words *Please, come.* When he shows up, he proves yet again why he was once my favorite person in the world. I guess he gets the details from my mom because when he comes into my room, he gives me a hug without even trying to kiss me. Quietly, he deals out some cards for crazy eights, which we play according to an elaborate set of rules and exceptions. When I say I don't feel like it he reshuffles and plays solitaire while I lie on the bed, not thinking.

Eventually, when it's really too dark and cold, he gets our coats and I follow him up Seventy-fourth Street to Lexington. We go to one of the coffee store chains that he hates and he buys me some kind of triple chocolate mocha that even I, with my endless sweet tooth, can't finish. We play tic-tac-toe, which stops being challenging after the age of seven, but is, weird-ly, always fun. After we have covered four sheets of paper in his notebook, Ben pushes it away and says,

"I really loved Rebecca."

I smile because I know exactly why he did. I didn't start Tyler Prep until eighth grade, and Ben was my first friend there. He was taking math and science classes with the eleventh-graders but also helping the sixth grade boys do things like rig the headmaster's office with water balloons. I liked how Ben fit in everywhere and nowhere. After he told our English teacher to stop calling on me to read aloud ("No sane person wants to do that," he said), we spent two years being best friends.

The summer before tenth grade, I went to stay with my grandparents in California and Ben went on a bik-ing tour of Spain with his older brother. When we got back to school, Ben was a complete psycho to me. I could not do or say anything right. We both almost got thrown off the tech crew for arguing so much.

I reported all of this to Rebecca, who gave me what I came to think of as *the look.* Sly, sweet, and amused.

"Ben wants to date you," she said. "He always has, but it took spending the summer with his hotshot brother to make him see it."

"What's his brother got to do with anything?"

"Ben has probably spent all summer explaining that yes, his best friend's a girl. No, he's not dating her. Yes, she's very pretty. No, there's nothing wrong with him."

I loved how Rebecca's voice slid over these imagined, ridiculous answers to stupid questions.

Hardly anyone at school ever dated. If you liked someone, you were supposed to hang out together with other people. But I had distinct memories of watching Rebecca get ready to go out with her husband when they were dating. It seemed like a good idea to have someone for whom it was worth taking the trouble to look nice.

"Well, why doesn't he just ask me, then?"

"Because Ben, while a really nice guy, is also a world-class geek," Rebecca said. "He doesn't know how."

I had already heard from her that most interesting men were geeks in high school. The more interesting the man, she said, the longer he had been a geek. And Ben, who collected maps, could take apart his father's computer, and wanted to be an architect, was the most interesting boy I knew. And the nicest. And, at the time, the most psycho.

"You have to ask him, nicely, if he wants to ask you out," my sister said. "Make it very clear you will say yes."

So I dutifully went off to tell Ben exactly what Rebecca had said, to which he replied, *Maybe I should ask* her *out*. But he settled for me and now everyone calls him my boyfriend and I suppose that fits; although I know he's something both more and less than that.

"I know you loved her," I tell him now.

"I kind of wish she'd been in a car wreck."

"I guess," I say, vaguely aware he has said something no one else will, but not sure that a car wreck would make anything easier.

Normally, Ben and I try to solve anything we think of as a problem together—that C in English, for example. Or when his mother got fired and didn't know how to tell his father. However, I'm not sure this qualifies as a problem. More to the point, I no longer want to solve problems with Ben.

Exactly five days ago, Ben and I decided, after months of my not being sure, that we should, no, make that we wanted to, have sex. For obvious reasons, this was not a decision I made only with him. I'm sure I love Ben enough and I know how my body feels with him. It feels the way I do with cake: I want more. But in this, as with cake, I didn't think more was exactly right.

And, so.

I asked my mother. I trust her more than almost

anyone else, and she has never lied to me. This time her answer was suspect.

"When you definitely want to, you'll know," she said.

"Doubt is your body's way of saying he's not the right one," she added. "Or that the time isn't right."

If it was up to my body, I'd have done it by now. Something I did *not* tell her but that she must have guessed.

"Honey, I'm not saying you're not ready," she said. "I just want you to honor your uncertainty."

She then went on to remind me of all the precautions I should take when and if Ben and I (or as she put it, *you and whoever*) went ahead. I didn't think she was lying, exactly, or that she was against it. But how would anyone ever face the first time of *anything* without being unsure?

A question I then took to Rebecca. This was back in August when Ben and I first started the *will we or not* talk. She laughed when I told her my mother's theory.

"That's so very Elsa," she said. "But look, you won't know until you do it. And, listen, I am not advocating reckless, mindless sex here."

I told her I'd already heard enough about preventing both pregnancy and disease.

"Of course you have," Rebecca said. "What I meant

is that Ben loves you and I think you're just scared. If after you do it, you still don't know what you want, then we'll have another talk."

I thought that a kind of truth lay somewhere between my mother and Rebecca. I spent a few months hoping to find it, but on the day before Thanksgiving my body decided what my brain was incapable of sorting out. It was more unpleasant than I had hoped. Not because it hurt, which it did, although a lot less than everyone says. What I didn't like was being the sole focus of Ben's attention while also feeling ignored.

This makes no sense, I know, but it's how it was. However, if it wasn't quite what I expected, it did at least shush the *more* feeling I always had when Ben and I pushed up against the limits of not doing it. I do a better job on my own, but that's got to be a practice thing.

Even after three more times with him, I still didn't know if I wanted to. This didn't make me sad or angry or disappointed—all things I suddenly feel now as I look at Ben and then down at the remains of my mocha. Rebecca promised me that we would talk, if after I slept with Ben I was still uncertain. Although maybe she thought he and I already had and that since I didn't say anything I was fine. But shouldn't she have checked with me before . . . ? Unless it was sudden.

Could overdosing on pills be a last-minute decision?

This is exactly the kind of confusion I need Rebecca to help me make clear. Not Ben. Even though it's typical of him to know things—important things—before I do. A car wreck, unless you are driving on purpose into a wall, is better than killing yourself. And yet, I've always checked his knowledge with someone I'm certain knows better.

There were many things Rebecca did tell me: why her parents divorced, why her own marriage ended, why I should be happy Janie was not my mother, and why Clare sought out the most unsuitable boyfriends. I thought of Rebecca as a living, breathing resource book for whatever was impossible to decipher on my own.

Everyone always complained that she was secretive. My mother had recently asked Da, after he'd had lunch with Rebecca, how she seemed, and if plans for expanding the store were going well. My father shrugged, saying,

"God forbid she tell me. She seems fine. Who knows? She looks good, though."

To which my mother said, "She always looks good. It's nice she called you."

Rebecca is easy to know, I remember thinking with a certain amount of *what is their problem.* And now I think how that lunch was only two weeks ago. The week before Thanksgiving. Oh, God. She can't have been fine. Even if she did decide to kill herself at the last minute, that kind of last-minute decision doesn't happen if you've been fine. Does it?

"My father," I say to Ben. "They just had lunch. He's never going to stop thinking he should have known."

"He'll think that anyway," Ben says. "Because of the first time, he's been worrying about this since forever."

Right, of course he has. I once told Janie that maybe Rebecca was so secretive because everyone tried to monitor her. I was going to present myself as living proof that if you didn't press Rebecca too hard for information, she'd part with it.

"Yes, she's given us such good reason not to keep an eye on her," Janie said dryly, and I just shut up. Whatever my sister had done to herself when she made those scars, she'd also done to her parents. And they hadn't gotten better.

"Let's get you home," Ben says. "I'll bring you your homework tomorrow."

"I'll be at school," I say, and then remember. How can I be forgetting the only thing I'm thinking about?

"I'm guessing you won't be," he says, helping me with my coat.

"I just never thought she would——" I say, before pulling the rest of that sentence in, far back in, never to see the light of day.

I'm not the one who gets to say I never thought she would leave me. Even if I am the only one who had that kind of faith in her. Just then I remember the one thing that people who kill themselves often do. It's the very thing that people in car wrecks can never do: write a note. There has to be one. One that explains.

She didn't leave me. Or if she has, she's left me with a story. There'll be a reason for all of this. I have to wait. Out of what seems, as Ben and I walk home, like an immense mess, there's an end. Dyslexia has taught me that clarity comes only through effort, patience, and help from those who know how to give it.

In many ways, I am uniquely qualified to discover why Rebecca has done this.

Four

THE PROCESS OF DISCOVERY is slowed to a grinding halt by all that needs to be done when someone dies. It seems wrong that such an event can be reduced to a series of chores, but there's clearly an ironclad set of rules here. We all line up to follow them.

At Rebecca's memorial service, which seems to take months of planning instead of the actual nine days, both Raphael Barclay and Clare's boyfriend wear the same tie. A black and gold checkerboard pattern masquerading as a splash of muted color. Although Gyula Rácz, who has been Clare's big love on and off for five years, is older and better-looking than Raphael, seeing them together makes me think that Clare has a type. I wish I could conjure up her boyfriend before Gyula. The one she lived with for a year and whom Da called a *vile example of humanity*.

I was barely eleven when they broke up and simply

not paying attention to anything about the woman I thought of as my *other* sister. I just don't know her, I realize now. I can see she's upset because of the death grip she has on Gyula's hand, but has she cried? At Janie's service, Rebecca and Da cried, but not Clare. So where does she go to do it? I wonder.

And, also, does she wonder the same thing about me, or has the distance between us simply grown wider without her noticing? Clare has recently grabbed my attention by leaving me off the list of people surviving Rebecca. Here, wrapped in stories I hardly know, is someone I should have thought to make important. Preferably before she went from being my *other* sister to my *only* one.

We got the programs—an idea I thought really smart at Janie's service and less fitting at this one—last night. Printed on the back, after information regarding *in lieu of flowers*, is *Rebecca Jane Abranel is survived by her father, Julian A. Abranel, her sister, Clare Lucie Abranel, her cousin Raphael Barclay, and her stepmother, Elsa Kent.* It's much worse, in my limited view, that William is not on this list. Divorced for four years maybe, but the service is at William's swanky club right off Park Avenue because finding available space in the city two weeks before Christmas isn't possible.

Da had a fit that there was no mention of *Leila Gwendolyn Abranel*. I couldn't believe he didn't see it as an accident.

"This is classic Clare," Da said. "Incredibly thoughtless and needlessly hard."

He continued on in this vein for some time until I pointed out the obvious.

"It's not like she did it on purpose," I said. "Clare doesn't know me well enough to dislike me. She's just stressed out."

My mother's not sleeping, Da's nose is bleeding almost every day, and I heard Raphael say he's got a headache no amount of aspirin can touch, so Clare's stress level is more than a guess. Add in some jet lag and it's clear how easy forgetting to put my name on a list might be. But my father didn't see it that way.

He put his head in his hands—he's doing that a lot when his nose isn't bleeding—and said, "That's very kind of you, Leila. You have such a big heart."

Da is always talking about what a big heart I have. At first, I thought it was only something he said when the girls were being particularly difficult, but eventually I came to see that he believed it. Personally, I think that what he calls a big heart is my inability to gather information easily. When you screw up your left and right, see letters backwards, and know you often make mistakes, it's easier to wait and see exactly what's what. Deciding quickly on an answer or conclusion—about anything—makes me wrong more than is already necessary.

It's possible Clare's whole purpose behind the program was to hurt my feelings, but I'd need to know a lot more before I decided that.

Thanks to Raphael and Gyula, I wind up spending most of the service thinking about men's ties. Mostly I think about them—picture them sliding under shirt collars and folding into perfect knots—as a way to avoid thinking about the best way to help my parents. They are going to have to go to Poland. They'll be gone about a year, but are still unsure of how to ask Clare if I can live with her while they're gone. Mom's not even sure that my living with Clare is a "workable" plan.

It's the only one we have, though, so it has to work.

Last year, my parents were offered positions on a team going to Poland to help create a state-of-the-art teaching hospital in Krakow. At first they were going to bring me along, but what with eleventh grade being so pivotal to college acceptance and my having dyslexia, that option was ruled out. Krakow, apparently, is not crawling with education specialists.

In June, they were still thinking about going and asked Rebecca if she could stay with me (the apartment she shared with Clare was too small for all three of us). I think my parents would leave me alone for a long weekend, but not a year. Rebecca was the clear choice as I'd spent most of fifth grade with her and William while my parents worked at a medical clinic in Africa. Da does a lot of this kind of work, including seven months at a refugee camp in Bosnia. Or in Serbia, but maybe it was Kosovo. Except that was, I think, later.

Keeping straight what happened when during that war is really hard for me. Da thought I wasn't paying attention until Rebecca pointed out that I'd only been six when the Bosnian war began. She told him to get over himself. I thought this was unkind, and to make up for it I started keeping a notebook of things I should know but don't. They're almost always things I overhear or read.

Write it down and figure it out later. That's something I can do.

Anyway, about Krakow Rebecca said, why not, she'd stay with me, but then they decided not to go. I'm pretty sure they will now. I've even told Mom that she should go ahead and call the hospital. Make the arrangements.

"Nothing's been decided yet, Leila," she said.

"He can't go alone," I said. "You have to go with him."

"Of course I do, but it's not so simple," she said. "Your happiness is important to us."

There was something so wrong about the word *happiness* in this particular conversation that we both fell silent. It was after midnight and it had been days since she'd told me not to stay up so late. I kissed her goodnight after deciding I would find a way to help them go to Poland. The problem they have leaving me with Clare hinges on how much she travels, for both work and Gyula. We are in need of a better plan, which is something my mother can usually devise without help.

My father can't stay here. It's out of the question. He can barely get out of bed. And when he can, his time is totally taken up being mad. He's beyond mad, actually. Volcanically angry is more like it.

It turns out that Rebecca didn't make a last-minute decision.

Back in August, she got the drugs she used to kill herself by writing prescriptions with Da's and William's

DEA numbers. This did not look good to the police, who were all over their offices. The hospital where they both work is considering an inquiry. There is, in all the questions, the idea that either Da or William gave Rebecca the information she needed.

"She was a hospice nurse," William apparently told the police. "She didn't need any help from us."

The police, or so Da told us, looked at them blankly. One of them flipped his notes back a few pages. "Thought she was a cook."

"Chef," Da corrected him. "Pastry chef. But she had been a hospice nurse."

I love this image of my father trying to improve the police's vocabulary, but the real point of the story, as even I can tell, is that Rebecca planned, for many months, to die. She used her own training against herself. She risked damaging reputations. She turned my father into someone who's exactly split between grief and rage.

I think that the more her death looks unforgivable, the more it seems obvious that she had cause—she had a reason—we haven't yet discovered. The note, which I had been so sure would explain, is of no help. Short, unaddressed, and left open on her desk, all it says is *Don't be sad. I really want to go.*

During October, she was in touch with people she hadn't seen in a long time. She even had lunch with William. If she went to the trouble of saying goodbye to everyone, she has to have had reason to leave. Something that made her do it.

I wish there were a way to explain this to Da. I think it would make him feel better to know why she did it, but maybe not. I don't feel better knowing Rebecca had a reason. It's more like I have a huge undone task: finding her story. Her why.

But first. Staring at Raphael and Gyula's ties has focused me. I know how to help my parents ask Clare to let me live with her. I pull William aside after the service, saying I need to talk to him. He takes me to the club's library, off-limits to nonmembers. I tell him about Poland. That my parents will be prevented from going by worrying about me.

"They have to go," I say. "They can't stay here."

"It's, um, well, the worst I've ever, um, seen him," William says, his small, fine hands gesturing into the air for no reason.

William is short and a little roundish and has, Da says, the wrong personality for a surgeon. But the right hands, I guess, because if you need a tumor removed,

William's the go-to guy. In spite of his being almost as old as Da, I always have trouble remembering how important William is at the hospital. He never acts like he's a big deal.

"Clare travels a lot," I say. "They won't be able to leave me only with her."

Not to mention she may tell them exactly where to go, but I am banking on Clare needing to feel useful. Since no one can do anything for her, she may be willing to be the one who does for others. Especially if she can split the job with someone else.

"Oh, Leila," William says. "Of course. I told you after the . . . you know, when your sister and I, um, well, when we separated. You always have a home with me."

In the library's dim light, I worry that he's about to cry, but probably not. It's been a while since I've been around a grown-up man who isn't weeping.

"I'd do anything, Leila," William says. "Not just for Julian. For you too."

Good. Because there's this one thing. Would he please tell my parents that he'd like to have me stay with him while my sister's away on business?

"It'll sound like a great idea if you bring it up," I say.

"Elsa's worried about leaving you," William says.

"A little," I say. "Yes."

"There will be pressure on them to stay," William says. "But every time he looks at you girls, all he sees is the one who's missing."

"He needs to be working," I say.

I have, over the years, heard Janie, Clare, Raphael, my mother, and most certainly Da talk about work as more than what they do to earn money. Clare is happy working. Mom and Raphael sound as if they feel safe in their labs. Da loves to find out what he still doesn't know about how people both fall sick and get well. Work is where they all go to be who they are.

"Of course he does," William says. "Remember the first thing Janie did when her illness began?"

I nod.

"If I'm working, I can beat this," Janie told my sisters when they tried to keep her from going to Berlin right after finding out she had cancer.

"Leila, he'll be okay," William tells me. "You mustn't let it weigh on you."

"Yes, right," I say, trying to avoid thinking the obvious: Barring accident or disaster, the next memorial service my family organizes will be for my sixty-seven-year-old father.

Da himself has to have sat through Janie's service

thinking that he would be next. Now burying Rebecca has made him—made all of us—feel that the end is that much closer.

Five

WILLIAM WORKS FAST and, as far as I can tell, soothes many of my mother's fears about leaving me behind.

I think he spent most of his energy convincing Mom, but even Da takes time from organizing notes and supply lists to listen in on my mother's discussion with me about their departure.

"You don't know Clare very well," Mom says. "It's almost as if you know William better than you know your sister."

I lived with him when I was in the fifth grade. I probably do know him better.

"Elsa, that's not right," Da says. "The girls love Leila."

The girls. I try sending my mother *be quiet* signals. This is just too hard for him. I look at Da, saying that

I'll be fine, of course I'll be fine. It's easier for me, I say, meaning easier than for Clare and him. Rebecca was my sister, yes, but not in a daily way. More like a special treat sister. I miss her, but not the way you'd miss air.

"A special treat," Da says, his voice and face both revealing that he hardly knows what he's saying. "I like that, a special treat."

He's an easier sell because he really has to go. He'll see what he needs to, and I was kind of counting on that. Mother's another story.

I like my mother. She's fair and reasonable and, when she chooses, funny. If I'd rather be like Janie, it's not because there's anything wrong with Mom. She wears pants she's had since medical school and really expensive jackets over men's shirts that are too big. She's as tall as I am (as Janie was) and her shoes, which have no heels, never look comfortable or stylish.

I like it that before my father, my mother's great love was her work and that what caught her attention was that Da needed her. This isn't anything she's told me, of course. But anyone could take the facts of my father's two marriages and put a story together. I may have put the story together incorrectly, but it's the one I like best. Mother helped Da use the pieces he had from his first life and they've built a whole new thing.

When the old thing (by which I mean Janie, Rebecca and Clare) bumps into her new thing, Mother makes it fairly smooth. So when she comes into my room as I am dressing to go out with Ben and says she wants to talk, I try to be as much like her as possible. She is, after all, someone who can build or fix almost anything.

"Let's assume Clare agrees to this," Mom says, getting right to the critical question.

I notice that no one has asked Clare since William talked to my parents. She's been over a few times. She and Da sit in the living room, combing through the details of Rebecca's plan. The drugs, the friends she saw, the hope to expand the store, what to do with the store. They go over everything except the *why*. For them, the *why* needs no discussion. They seem to feel that the way Rebecca died was as much a part of her as her height and her collection of silk scarves.

Clare's lost weight since returning from Budapest, something she hardly needs to do. When my mother asked if she was eating, my sister shrugged, saying, "Oh, you know. At work, they say I treat grief like a diet."

"Clare will agree," I say to my mother now. "She'll want to do this for Da."

"Assuming she does," Mom repeats. "It's going to

be very hard for you. Harder than you're thinking."

"I *am* thinking it'll be hard," I say. "But not impossible."

"It's not being with Clare that will be hard," my mother says. "Clare is a remarkable person."

I think that's probably right even if she's a remarkable person I hardly know.

"It's more that eventually you're going to feel as though I chose your father over you," Mom says. "That I thought of him more."

"I'm not," I say. "I'm not going to think that."

And so what if I do? I don't have to be a genius to know she can't be in two places at once. I'll get over it.

"You might, Leila, and it's normal. All I want to say is that when it happens, please know I'm sorry. You'll be right to be angry, but never think this was an easy choice."

For as much as I like my mother (and I love her too, of course, but everyone loves their mother, that's no accomplishment), her insistence on not only telling me what I will think but also trying to shape the outcome of those thoughts makes me very uncomfortable.

"Okay," I say. "I won't."

I still have to put my hair up and pick out a

sweater. My mother and I consider each other. She is not as easy to lie to as Da is. But if I tell her I think Clare is a stranger and that I'm worried about Da's dying, I will only make this next year that much more difficult for her.

"People will judge him," Mom says. "I guess I want you to know it's okay if you blame us too."

"Judge him for what?" I ask, wondering if that's what William meant when he said there would be pressure on my parents to stay.

"People think they know what they would do if their—if their child died," Mom says. "They think they wouldn't go off."

I wonder if she has anyone in mind. How dare anyone think badly of my father. Let them come live here for a day and then tell me what he *should* do. That's ridiculous.

"This is the right choice," I tell her, wanting to say that she of all people is beyond being judged. "It really is."

Da needs a new way to keep busy while he gets used to this sudden gaping hole.

"Yes," Mom says. "Okay. Well."

It's still preying on her, I can tell. The idea that whatever she does will be the wrong thing. Mom was almost forty-one when she had me. She didn't grow up wanting to become a mother so much as an interesting person. As a result, she's never tried to treat me the way she thinks a mother *should*. She treats me, instead, like one of the most important people in her life.

I think it's one of the reasons we get along so well. It's always been my plan to someday repay her for letting me know how much I matter. If I could convince her that I understand why she and Da are leaving, I could get a start on that repayment.

I've imagined a variety of ways of how I'm going to wind up. How things conclude. The end of my particular story. They involve at least one great love—some perfect blend of William and Gyula Rácz. A career in the theater, the details of which are still murky except for my neither acting in plays or writing them. But however things settle, one thing is completely clear to me.

I'm not going to blame my parents for doing what was necessary.

My mother's still here, so while I am making a French braid, I tell her a little about my plans. I leave out the perfect love stuff and don't make the theater sound like a done deal because that's not what they want for me. But I spell out the not blaming them part and I guess I do it well, because by the time I'm ready to put on earrings, she kisses the top of my head, says, *Thank you, Leila,* and goes out, shutting the door softly behind her.

I'm late to meet Ben and we barely make it to the theater. Da got the tickets for this ages ago, when it opened. It's about a man and a woman trying to find their drug-addict father. Even though I don't like the play as much as the acting, it's nice to be doing something normal with Ben. I just wish I knew how to tell him that we're not having sex again anytime soon. Maybe I'll figure it out by the time my parents go to Poland. When I know where I'll be living.

In the end, my parents don't ask Clare anything and I get another lesson in how information flies around Julian Abranel's first family.

William, who knows Clare can't stand him, calls Raphael to get help in brokering a truce. William tells Raphael he wants it to be easy for Clare to be in touch with him during the year my parents are in Poland. Raphael, who has always loved Clare in one way or another, calls her to see what he can do to help.

"Help with what?" she asked, hoping he wasn't going to offer, once again, to close and sell Rebecca's store.

"Well, you know," he said. "When Julian and Elsa leave Leila with you and William."

I try to picture Clare, on the phone, absorbing the news. The phone has not been good to her recently. After Da called her in Budapest, I'm surprised she still picks up anything that rings.

Clare and Raphael have dinner at his house. They do not discuss the store, although Clare does, I will learn later, tell him that she can't stop wishing Rebecca had left instructions for it instead of *that stupid, useless note.* For the most part, my sister and her cousin avoid the recent death in the family and work out a plan where I will live with Clare, but stay with Raphael when Clare is traveling.

Raphael calls William. Who calls Da. Who tells me.

"Raphael is devoted to your sisters," Da says. "He's turned out quite well when you consider how God-awful his father was."

"I like Raphael," I say.

I know William better, but whatever. The year ahead of me will be Rebecca's doing, and she would pick Raphael over William. So.

"Clare can be very hard," Da says. "She'll never forgive William, and this does make everything easier."

"Forgive him for what?" I ask. "What did William do?"

Normally, when asked, Da isn't a good source of information about the girls. He doesn't know, can't recall, or won't say. Caught off-guard, however, he'll cough up a lot.

"He wanted Rebecca to have a baby," my father says, and something in his eyes makes me vow never again to point him in the direction of this memory.

This can't possibly be why Clare can't stand William. Everyone knew Rebecca didn't want children. From way before marrying William. There's got to be more than one missing detail in the he-wanted-a-baby account.

"I was at Raphael's a couple of years ago," I say. "He had a housewarming party when he moved to Brooklyn."

Rebecca took me because Clare wouldn't go. Raphael lives in a brownstone he's renovated that's about a block from the Brooklyn Heights Promenade. The Promenade, with its black iron fence, pretty buildings on one side, huge view on the other, and cobbled walkway in between, used to be one of my favorite places to visit. But now it's just a place from which it's possible to see (with a sick clarity) exactly how the city was attacked. I won't be going to the Promenade when at Raphael's.

At school, there are two types of people. People like Ben, who know everything about the attacks, down to the names of all nineteen hijackers. And people like me, who simply can't think about it. I went down there, of course. You had to look and whisper that you were sorry even if only your heart heard it. And I made myself stand on Fifth Avenue by Washington Square Park and stare at how nothing rose through the park's archway.

Everything about that day is bigger than I can hold on to. People say that knowledge is power. (This is actually something teachers say. And certain posters at the library.) Normally, I agree, but not about that day. I'm almost grateful to the dyslexia because I don't think I could get on a plane to Poland. Even to help Da.

I look at my father and think about Raphael and his house. I can learn to like him as much as I do William.

"Clare's invited us over," Da says. "For New Year's. Raphael, too. She thinks you should have the chance to spend time with them. Before you have to."

Da always makes a big fuss over New Year's Day because of our having no other end-of-the-year holiday. Clare would often come over with presents and a good mood (and sometimes with a boyfriend, but mostly not). Rebecca never came, saying she couldn't possibly make plans so far in advance.

"Decide at the last minute," Da might say.

It's not like we did much—just wore nice clothes and had a fancy meal with cheese and sorbet courses. Lots of different forks and linen napkins.

"I can't," she said. "If I came even once, it would feel like I was obliged for every year."

At the time, I thought this made Rebecca extra dazzling. Now that she will never come to anything again, I guess I think she should have erred on the side of obligation.

Six

ON NEW YEAR'S DAY, Da and I arrive at Clare's just as Raphael does. Early, as it turns out, since my sister is still in her pajamas. They're like men's pajamas, except the pants taper at the ankle and the buttons on her shirt are made of shells. The pattern, which I can't help staring at, is of different pieces of sushi. Like the place mats at a Japanese restaurant.

"You look like a menu," Da says.

"Thank you," Clare says, her voice at once amused and irritated. "Such charm before I've even had my coffee."

"You look beautiful," Raphael says. "I'll make the coffee—I brought a lot to cook and I can get it started."

He does have a bag of groceries, which he carries into the small kitchen I first saw when Janie lived here.

"I forgot you don't cook," Da says.

"I'm such a disappointment," Clare says, although I know Da didn't mean it like that.

It's more that Rebecca was a great cook and I can manage well enough. My father just forgot that Clare doesn't go on the *copes well in kitchen* list.

"Well, I'm sure I don't think that, and besides, Raphael's right, you do look beautiful," Da says, holding his coat and standing in the middle of the living room.

And she does, actually, although I never think of her that way. In addition to being thin, Clare is tall with wide shoulders and very long blonde hair just like Janie's. Like Mom's, actually. Like mine. It's always been interesting to me that while Clare and I are related because of Da, we look a lot alike because of our mothers. Janie, while mostly different from Mom, looked like her. Rebecca used to say that Da clearly had a type.

"How boring is blonde?" she'd ask and then shrug if Clare said, *Hey, watch it.*

"Being blonde is not all it's cracked up to be," Janie once told me. "People think you're dumb and your skin goes to hell faster."

That and people always ask if it's real and then want to see your scalp before they'll believe you. That bothers me.

I don't mind the dumb part (people think what they think), but I'm still a little worried about my skin going to hell. My mother, when asked, shrugged, saying, *I guess.* Her looks are not a top concern—she gets her soap from the grocery store. Rebecca used to give me bottles of a French face cleanser she used. *In a few years, I'll turn you over to Clare,* she said. *I don't know what to do with all that pale skin.*

Rebecca was the dark one, with a small, curvy body and black, black hair. She looked like one of the Abranel girl cousins in old photographs taken before the lost hotels were lost. Rebecca looked beautiful. Clare, except for this morning with her tired eyes and tangled hair, always looks prepared and deeply occupied with the task at hand.

Normally, you don't think *beautiful* when you look at Clare. Instead you wonder what she's thinking.

She takes our coats and says she's sorry she's not dressed.

"Gyula's here," she says, accepting a cup of coffee from Raphael, who also gives one to Da. "He took me out to dinner last night, late. I don't even want to think what he tipped to get us in with no reservation."

"You went out to dinner?" Da asks. "You and Gyula?"

"It was after this enormous party with every Hungarian in the city," Clare says. "Like going to Budapest without flying."

"You don't like to eat out," Da says.

This is a chronic complaint of his about Clare: that she won't sit over a meal. That she's thinking of the check as soon as she arrives. I've eaten out with Da a lot and I totally see Clare's point. He can take hours.

"I don't," Clare says. "But Gyula thought it was important to be here for me. And this is how he does things. Big and his way."

"Leila, what if I make you some hot chocolate?" Raphael asks.

"Yes," I say. "Thank you."

I should offer to help him, I know, but looking at Clare like this, all curled up in the sofa, holding her coffee cup and freely offering details of her private life, is like meeting someone again for the first time. It's impossible, but it's happening.

"I'd like to give Leila her things," Da says, and I freeze, looking to my sister to see if this moment has been ruined, but she nods.

"Okay, sure," she says. "I think they're probably in her bedroom. Feel free to look."

Rebecca left me some things in her will. In an

addendum or codicil or something she had drawn up in August right around the time she got her drugs. A bracelet that had been given to her by one of Da's aunts, a cashmere shawl, and some photographs.

"It's not much," Da told me. "But they're now yours."

If she took the trouble to leave me things, why wasn't I one of the people she saw in the few weeks before she did it? In the past month, I've had these bouts of . . . well, of wanting to smack Rebecca right across the face. And then the stupidity of this thought or desire or whatever it is makes my head want to explode.

I'm not mad she did it. It's more that by doing it, she became more of the person Da and Clare know. Less of the one I thought I did. I have to figure this out. If only I knew why she did this. Why would anyone do this? I mean, really.

"In the bedroom?" Da asks. "Have you been in there?"

"Yeah, yes, sure, of course," Clare says. "Door's open, bed's made. Go on, I'll keep Leila company."

There's no mistaking my sister's grim satisfaction in sending Da into Rebecca's room. Da looks reluctant but walks off in that direction. I think that while Clare understands why Da is going away, she's not that happy with his decision. But I could be wrong, as she smiles at me in a real enough way.

"The photographs are over there," she says, motioning to the windows. "I'm pretty sure those are the ones she meant for you to have."

Three frames hang between the windows. Here they are: the lost hotels.

"The two on the left are of the Barcelona one and the other is Alexandria."

Hearing Clare say the city's name is like magic. She obviously knows far more about it than I do. Da always says that if his city had once belonged to the world, now it's just another part of Egypt. When he lived there, Alexandria was almost a part of Europe.

Or, as Da would put it, *We made the mistake of believing it was.* In the years before he left, street and store names were changed from French, Italian, or Greek into Arabic. No one knew where anything was. They'd lost the city while still living in it. By now it has slipped away so thoroughly that even if I managed to go there, I wouldn't be at the place where he grew up.

But Clare says its name as if it's still a tangible place. As if she knows it.

"I thought these were yours," I say, looking away from the windows to the couch.

"My copies are at my office," she says. "Rebecca always said you loved them."

"Yes," I say, and then, testing what is possible, what is allowed, add, "It's more that I'm curious. About them."

"Sure," Clare says. "Of course."

"Do you know a lot?" I ask. "About when Da lived there."

"Some," she says.

"Do you know why they stayed so long?" I ask.

That's the bit I always return to. Da's family left more than a year after almost every other Jewish family had cleared out. By the time Da got to Paris, his memories of Alexandria weren't all good.

"I can guess," Clare says, smiling at Raphael, who has come back in to give me hot chocolate. "Uncle Jacques was buried there."

"In the Jewish cemetery," I say to show that there are some things I know.

"I think it must have been hard to leave him behind," Clare says.

Jacques was my father's brother. The one who drowned. The one married to Aunt Ingrid. I look at Raphael, realizing that without the drowning he wouldn't be here. He's the result of a ruined love, just as I am. I wonder what else I'll figure out this year without even trying.

"It's nice," I say, wincing at how lame the word is. "That you can both do this. Have me, you know."

"It is," Raphael says. "It will be."

"You'll have my room," Clare says. "I'm going to set something up in here. Don't worry."

Which is not exactly saying that she thinks it'll be nice, but . . . I definitely don't want to sleep in Rebecca's room. Clare's looking toward the narrow hallway where the bedrooms are, and we can hear the sound of voices. Gyula's up and talking to Da. They come in to the living room together.

Gyula kisses both sides of my face and shakes Raphael's hand. Da hands me the bracelet and tells Clare he can't find the shawl.

"We think it's being, how-do-you-say-it, dry-cleaned," Gyula says. "But there's no ticket. She's looked."

Rebecca used to say that Gyula spoke better English than any American and that the whole search for the right word was an act. Maybe. But it's one I've always liked.

"I'll pick it up," Clare says. "But they'll ask after her, I know it."

"Clare's plan is to change all her places," Gyula says. "Cleaners, stores, restaurants."

He says it kindly and he clearly admires her for this ability to protect herself, but it's equally clear my sister wishes he had not chosen to share her plan with all of us.

"I'll go," Raphael says. "Dry cleaners don't need a slip, just the phone number."

"You will?" Clare asks. "Really?"

"I know where it is."

I'm watching Gyula, as he's endlessly handsome and I've spent five years staring at him while wishing I could stop. Right now, as I watch him look at the other two, I think that if this were a play and I were building the set, I would start with Gyula. I would take his silence here and move out from it, as Janie recommended.

This is a really bad habit of mine. When I am nervous or not quite sure of what I'm doing, I turn life into a play. I try to imagine the people around me with stage directions and the set they might need. It does calm me down and help me think. But it also makes me feel a little freakish.

I put on the bracelet, which is a wide and heavy gold band with emeralds on either side. I've never seen it before.

"It's more valuable than attractive," Da says to me

before turning to Clare, something else in his hand. "I want to give this to Leila. She's sixteen, just like Rebecca was."

It's the ring his mother gave him before he got married. I know the story behind this, at least. It was for Julian to give to Janie, but she never wore it and so he decided, when Rebecca was born, that she should get it for her sixteenth birthday.

"Yes," Clare says. "Of course."

"I think you should have it," I say. "You were sixteen before me."

The ring is slender and gold. It holds three small diamonds in separate settings and looks, for all the world, like an engagement ring.

"No," Clare says. "I'm pretty sure she'd want you to have it."

Which is how my father comes to give this ring, for the second time, to his sixteen-year-old daughter. I know I will wind up keeping it on a ribbon hanging in my closet. I'd wear it if it had come from Rebecca. But almost better than that, better than even wearing it, is Clare's belief that it should be mine. I now own something that has traveled from the Alexandrian Abranels through the Julian and Janie Abranels. To me. The Leila kind.

Seven

MY PARENTS LEAVE A WEEK LATER but I manage to get homesick *before* they go. I haven't even moved to Clare's yet, but the cold, hollow place in my chest that I remember from summer camp roars into place. It's the cat's fault.

The cat—skinny, with gray stripes and named My Scott—was a gift last year from Rebecca. My Scott had been hers—he was a gift from a friend when she and William divorced. She had him for three years, but Clare's allergic and Janie's rent-controlled apartment is in a building that doesn't allow them. So I kind of inherited him when the girls moved in together. I'm not really a cat person so much, but I respect the way he ignores me unless I'm busy. I also like how he falls asleep on places most likely to resent having cat hair all over them.

Ben's taking him. Mrs. Greene, who mostly thinks

I'm a bad influence on her sainted son, was great about allowing it. Ben says his mother is totally spooked about Rebecca's death and keeps saying, *Oh, that poor man. That poor family.* She's taking my cat, so it's kind of hard to resent her pity.

I leave My Scott at Ben's along with the carrier, toys, a stash of catnip, and a long list of instructions.

"Oh, my God," Ben says. "Are you kidding me?"

"He was Rebecca's," I say in what I hope will be a voice stern enough to keep my real thoughts—*I'm going to miss my parents*—hidden and quiet.

"He's not going to die on my watch," Ben says. "I promise."

This is all very nice of Ben, as he and I have just broken up. The idea of telling Ben that I wasn't sure I wanted to keep on sleeping with him seemed both horrible and impossible. Not to mention unkind. It felt easier to say I was too focused on family stuff to be a good girlfriend. Ben asked if I meant Rebecca and I nodded. After all, in a way this was her fault. If she weren't dead, I'd have been able to ask her what to do. Ben took a few days to think about it and then told me that only a jerk would expect me not to feel differently about a lot.

"It doesn't matter," he said. "As long as we're still

friends. The other stuff doesn't matter."

Maybe he's been as uncertain as I have about wanting to have sex. This is upsetting for reasons that I can't quite sort out.

"Here's the only thing," Ben said. "If you start dating someone else, you tell me. Even if it's not someone at school. I get to know first."

It sounded like an order, but okay. While I like almost everyone at school, only Ben, who is heading to M.I.T. and yet never makes me feel stupid, is what I would call my friend. There are other people I like, but only Ben is important. I'd do a lot for us to stay that way. Almost anything except sleep with him again. So I told him I would tell him first. And that my dating anyone else seemed highly unlikely.

I scratch My Scott's head while taking a look around Ben's room. In spite of its plaid wallpaper and the toy car collection, I like it here. It is, after all, the place where I've done math homework, had sex, and drawn up blueprints. It's the only place that makes me glad I have to be in school. Without school, I wouldn't know Ben.

"Thank you," I say. "It's nice to think of My Scott being here."

"You can come see him whenever you want," Ben says.

The cat will be gone, but available. Unlike my parents, who will be really and truly gone. I hug Ben, press my nose into My Scott's fur, and wave goodbye to Mrs. Greene. Rebecca seems to be the only person I can miss right now. I can't—or won't—let myself wish I still had my cat, my parents, or my boyfriend exactly as I once did.

In fact, it's only the cat's goodbye which I allow to stay with me. Not the one with my parents, the details of which I cannot recall other than the obligatory whispered *I love you, be good, be safe, don't worry, bye.* Goodbye.

Clare does her crying at night and in the bathroom. I find this out immediately. She runs all the faucets and flushes over and over. But even with that, I can hear the distinct sound of sobbing. It's not that I'm listening for it so much as why else would anyone hole up in the bathroom in the middle of the night?

The bathroom, which has an enormous tub, wicker shelves, and an ugly tiled floor, is between the bedrooms. Clare has cleared out the front hall closet so I can use the one in her room and she has bought Japanese screens and a dresser for the living room. She takes cushions off the sofa and makes it up every night with a fitted sheet.

"There's no greater luxury than clean sheets," she tells me. "And now I have them all the time."

"Like at a hotel," I say.

"There's nothing like a hotel here," she says. "When Gyula comes back to town, we'll have dinner at his place. Now, that's like a hotel."

Gyula doesn't especially like it here and since Rebecca couldn't stand him, he never used to stay with Clare, preferring an apartment he rents in a hotel on Central Park South. New Year's was a one-time-only exception. I have the distinct impression that he's not anxious to sleep in the living room on an old couch. I try to tell Clare that I would happily give her the bedroom when Gyula's visiting.

"Don't give it a thought," she says. "He'll never sleep with me while there's a minor in the house."

Sleep with me. I mean, of course I know. I've just never had to know and hear it specifically said all at once. Although, she's not even talking about sex, but about her boyfriend's scruples. Which is funny since both Da and Rebecca would go on and on about how unlikely it was for an ex–Communist Party official to build his fortune honestly. They thought he was a liar and probably a thief. Someone with no scruples.

And yet Clare loves him. Sleeps with him. Probably

knew right away that she wanted to sleep with him.

"I could, you know, go to Raphael's," I say. "You know, when Gyula, well, is, um, here."

God, could I stammer around the topic any more? Sometimes I am the most immature person I know.

"Maybe," Clare says. "If I spend the night at the hotel, you'll have to go to Brooklyn. I'm not leaving you here alone."

"You could," I say, pretty confident I won't start a fire if unsupervised.

"Not going to happen," she says with a laugh. "You too have a boyfriend."

"Had," I remind her.

Clare had been really sweet when I told her Ben and I weren't dating anymore. She didn't ask any questions other than was I okay. She said going back to being friends was often a good idea and that she'd had more than one boyfriend she wished she'd done that with.

"Even so," she says now, "these things have a way of changing and I'm under strict instructions not to make anything too easy for him."

I don't have anything to say to that and so we mercifully drop the whole subject of who is and isn't sleeping with whom. I wish I knew her well enough to tell her what I never got the chance to tell Rebecca.

That everyone in the world could make it *too easy* for Ben and me (as his parents did many times by leaving us alone in their apartment), but that I still wouldn't know if I wanted to do that easy thing. Sex with Ben made my body briefly peaceful, but my thoughts a constant mess. If I could tell her that, would Clare be able to help?

On the fifth night of listening to my sister's water show, I make a cup of tea and leave it in front of the bathroom door. I hear the spoon clink against the cup when Clare comes out and then she knocks on my door.

"Thanks," she says. "Did I scare you?"

"No," I say. "But I thought maybe it would help you sleep."

"Maybe," Clare says.

"You don't have to go in there," I say. "I mean, I'm not going to get upset . . . you know, it's your house. You can do it in the living room."

"I'm not hiding from you, Leila," she says. "It's—I can't stand the sound. It's like snot pouring out of your eyes. It's gross."

Da doesn't cry like that. He sounds like someone with an empty stomach being forced to throw up and breathe all at the same time.

"I remember this from when Mama died," Clare says, leaning against my—her—desk. "This crying like it'll never stop. But it's better than the surprise kind that shows up whenever. Like at the office."

Yes, I can see that. I wouldn't want to go to school worried about breaking down in front of everyone. Even though they've all been careful to let me know how sorry they are. And no one would mind or be surprised if I suddenly had hysterics in the middle of math class. No one at Clare's office would mind either, but I think it's more that the kind of crying she's doing—the kind Da did—is private.

I'm not doing it, which is nice in a way, but I wonder if it means I loved Rebecca less than Clare and our father did. A thought to push away. This is what Mom meant about people judging Da for going to Poland. We all think there's just one right way to fall apart. Da and Clare have their way and I'll find mine.

"It's nice tea," Clare says. "What is it?"

"There were some dried chamomile flowers in the cabinet above the stove," I say. "I put them in that mesh thing, poured hot water and added a whole lot of honey."

"God," Clare says, laughing. "I can't remember the last time anyone went to that kind of trouble for me."

"Rebecca used to make me flower tea," I say and then want to bite down on the insides of my mouth until a river of blood pours out.

"Right, right," Clare says. "All the tea stuff is hers. The pot, though, that's mine. I had it in law school, although I didn't use it. My mother drank a lot of tea. I mean, you know, being English, of course she did. But I like coffee, except when it's late. This is perfect."

"I'm glad," I say as my heart beats out, *I am so sorry.*

It's a measure of comfort that Clare doesn't go back into the bathroom when she backs out of the room. And while I wish I hadn't dragged Rebecca's name into the night, I feel a little less lonely on the next night and on each one after. I know Clare's in there so snot can run out of her eyes and she knows I know. It's not the greatest of bonds, but it's a start.

Eight

MY SISTERS DID A GREAT JOB of making this apartment theirs after Janie died, but Clare has yet to make it hers alone. For a while, I keep feeling as if I'm only visiting and that any minute Rebecca will walk in, apologize for being late, and ask how my day is going. I sometimes go into Rebecca's room to check that she's not just napping.

I know she's not, of course, but the checking makes me feel better. Also worse. And freakishly crazy until Clare mentions that she sometimes dials Rebecca's work number.

"It's partly habit," Clare says. "And partly I want her to be there enough to settle for remembering the number."

Even at school, I find myself thinking of and looking for Rebecca. I hadn't realized how much of a lie I told Da. Yes, Rebecca was like a special treat to me, but I'm used to having special treats fairly often. Although I didn't see her as regularly as I might have a "real" sister, thinking of her was, it turns out, a daily occurrence. Just never before in a classroom or locker-lined hallway.

Other than seeing Ben or occasionally beating my dyslexia enough to understand homework, school's not a place where interesting things happen. By surfacing here, Rebecca is demanding both my attention and my interest. Well, not Rebecca, obviously, but the story she's left for us. Left for me.

I can't decide what to think about not being one of the people Rebecca saw for a last time as she was making her goodbyes. The people on that list must have received the news of her death with anxious thoughts about their last meeting with her. Was there something they should have said or done differently? Would she have changed her mind if they had known to try?

I wouldn't want to have to ask those questions. After all, what would I have said to Rebecca if I'd known about her plan? *Please don't?* I hope someday I'll arrive at a better answer than that.

I'm probably glad I didn't have the chance to regret everything I did or didn't say. But not being picked for a final farewell brings its own doubts. Who were these people she selected and what made them valuable? My being passed over could be proof of my unimportance or could be, instead, one more thing I'll never know.

In the hopes of finding clues or answers, I endlessly review the last two times I saw her.

In September, probably near Labor Day, she closed the store early and came uptown for dinner. There was no discussion that night of *Islam, Taliban,* or *Pashtuns,* whose definitions I have since hunted down. So I'm thinking early September, but I wasn't paying enough attention at the time to say for sure.

Rebecca brought us a box of small chocolate pastries and told me, no, I would not look good with bangs. That neither my hair nor my personality was suited to them. I think I left before she did so I could meet Ben for a movie. I would have said something along the lines of *Hey, thanks for the cake. See you later.*

I didn't see her in a planned way after that, which was unusual, but not unheard of. I knew she was hoping to expand her store and was therefore super busy. Also, October was the one-year anniversary of Janie's death and I could count on the remaining three members of Janie and Julian's family to be distant and bummed out.

The second time also involves pastry, but has more to do with chance than with Rebecca.

My tutor lives in a walkup apartment on one of those small streets tucked between Bleecker and West Fourth. Right opposite the apartment there's a café, and whenever I pass it I look through the windows to the pastry case in the back. I promise myself that when I am free (of school, learning disorders, and the chronic fear which comes from both), I will stop there every afternoon. I have been passing this café twice a week for almost four years.

Being able to stop there for no reason has gradually become a part of how I picture the way I'll wind up. The café scenario is almost more important than the career in theater, having a great love, and never blaming my parents for what they've had to do.

The dyslexia's not a problem in this picture, and I have a book with me that's difficult to read but that I understand. I'm not reading, but having the book is important. I'm with someone (I think a man, but that's not as clear as the book) and between us on a round, glass plate is a napoleon: flaky and sweet. There's also, next to the plate, a scallop-edged paper napkin and a small fork. This last bit is important, as it's the details that make or break a fantasy.

And it was here, intruding upon my vision of the future, that I last saw my sister.

I was passing Caffe Acca, looking into it from across the street, when I registered that the woman seated in the window was Rebecca. It was close to five and the light spilled out from the café into the surrounding shadow. It was like looking at a stage with all of the figures thrown into clear relief. I stopped rushing, so as to see what was really there.

My sister was facing a man whose face was obscured by a tall green fern. I could see his body behind the plant's slender stalk. He was thin and wearing dark pants. I stood still on the other side of the street, just looking.

Rebecca was leaning forward, with her hands clasped together and the tips of her index fingers pressed against her lips. Her profile looked fragile and glowing against the surrounding wood panels and lights. If the man's body hadn't been so thin, I might have wondered if she was with William. When the man reached out and ran his fingers along her arm, I decided it definitely wasn't William. She looked down at the hand, up at the man, and then away.

More than away. Out. Out through the window. Out through the window to me.

Her expression didn't really change and for a second I thought perhaps she didn't see me. But she brought her hands up to her face so that it was shielded from the man in front of her.

This is it, I thought. She's going to send me some kind of a message. Was she mad that I had seen her? I waited for what was probably no more than a moment, but seemed forever before she moved a hand in front of her face. The fingers actually. She was waving at me.

I just stood there trying to guess at her meaning. Then her lips moved and she mouthed a word at me. Words? I couldn't tell. I looked from her face to her hand. I lifted my own hand to wave back. Rebecca shrugged and turned back to the man at her table.

Right then he leaned forward and I thought I recognized him. His hair was dark and his face, at least in profile, was taken up by his nose and mouth. I decided he was simply familiar in the way that all good-looking people are. And yet, I really wanted to know him. Wanted to rush in and ask, *Who are you?*

Because Rebecca had a history of craving privacy as

if it were a drug, I mostly kept a studied indifference toward things she chose to hide: boyfriends, vacation plans, and on occasion, her whereabouts. On the street that day, I decided I was more afraid of infuriating her than I was curious about the man. I touched my waving hand to my face and the unexpected cold it held made me wonder where I had stashed my gloves at the end of last winter.

As I turned away and made a left onto Bleecker, I thought that perhaps I had misunderstood what I wished for. Maybe I didn't want a book I could read or a man who might be my great love. Maybe I wanted to sit and split a pastry with Rebecca. Had there been a pastry on the table? I put the whole thing out of my mind as I went home. Someday, after all, I would sit and split a pastry with her. I had, in fact, already done so. Many times. It was unlikely that such a common occurrence would find its way into my fantasy of the future.

And yet.

As sitting with Rebecca turns itself into a strictly past-tense event, I find myself returning over and over to that moment outside of Caffe Acca. I can't make myself stop, although there are better, longer memories I could dwell on. Memories where I do more than watch her through a window.

It takes me a while to guess. It isn't whether or not she had a pastry that's important; the detail that counts is the possibility she was waving goodbye.

Nine

AFTER I PUT TOGETHER that Rebecca's *goodbye* happened without my realizing it, I try being extra kind, polite and patient with everyone I see. People on the bus, my math teacher, and even the seventh grade boys who voted me most-fun-to-look-at. I usually go out of my way to ignore them (I mean, gross), but you just never know. It could be the final time I see any of them.

Only this doesn't last long, as it's not possible to get out of bed while remembering that for someone, somewhere, this is it, the end of the story. Eventually, brushing my teeth and finding a sharp pencil become more important. In fact, my brain is so foggy lately that it's amazing I remember half of what I need to in order to navigate my days. If my being so clueless were happening to someone else, I'd find the things

I'm failing to see (to know, remember, and under-stand) kind of hilarious.

They're big, red flag kinds of things.

For example, it's suddenly impossible to care about stage sets. The drama club is putting on *The Children's Hour* for the Spring Arts Festival. I read the play several times last year and had been looking forward to building sets of the plush library and the grim sitting room that would be required. I had thought of a big bay window for the grandmother's house and narrow shuttered windows for the teachers accused of being lesbians.

Now, I simply sit through crew meetings wondering why anyone would want to see this play. Can it be worth an entire evening? Even with three changes of scenery? And then suddenly, the deal an audience makes with the actors (where everyone pretends that what's happening is real) strikes me as silly. And a waste of time.

"And I used to think it was so interesting," I say to Raphael. "The way the audience *and* the actors pretend different things for the same reason."

"For the sake of the play," Raphael says. "Is that what you mean?"

"Yes," I say. "That's exactly what I mean."

"It sounds like you still think it's interesting," he says.

"I guess," I say. "I just don't want to build these sets."

"*The Children's Hour* is about more than a false accusation, right?" Raphael asks. "Isn't there a suicide at the end?"

"Offstage," I say. "At the very end. The teacher who believes the lie the most. She blows her brains out."

"That's what I thought," Raphael says. "Pass me that, will you?"

We are making salad and I hand him the bowl of cucumber slices, and then—not immediately but after a bit—I put down the knife I am using to chop spinach.

"Oh," I say. "Of course. She kills herself at the end."

"Maybe it's not the right play for you just now," he says.

I watch him make a couple of flower-shaped radishes.

"Maybe not so much," I say.

Raphael is staying with me for a few days. He and Clare have decided that when she's away for work, I go to Brooklyn. When she's away because Gyula's in town, Raphael comes to the apartment and sleeps in the living room.

"She already feels bad about how much disruption

you have," Raphael said when he explained who would go where, when, and why.

I suspect that Clare feels guilty about how often she is away. Raphael says that she thinks I've had entirely too many people leave me recently. Since she can't prevent the travel for work, she thinks she shouldn't also leave to be with Gyula. I actually think that's the best reason of all. It seems fitting that Clare and Gyula should meet only in hotels or in what I imagine is his large and elegant Budapest apartment.

"It's fun being at your place," I tried telling Raphael in an effort to go to Brooklyn when my sister is with her boyfriend. "I like it."

And I do. Raphael is still fixing up his third floor and I love how there's a bathroom with no floor or shower and two rooms littered with sawdust and tools. Although, I have to say that when Raphael is at Clare's, his presence removes how much Rebecca still lingers in the apartment. Seeing his shaving stuff in the bathroom makes me happy. But guilty too. That he's had to pack it all up and bring it here.

"Clare's life with Gyula is already complicated," Raphael said when I asked again if he didn't think I should come to Brooklyn. "It's easier for her if I am the one moving around. That way she doesn't have to feel she's putting you out of your bed."

I've already put Clare out of *her* bed. I looked at Raphael, waiting for him to make some sense.

"So to speak," he said.

Okay, then. "Well, she's putting you out of yours," I said.

"In her mind, she still owes you," he told me.

From things they've both said, I know that Clare views herself as having been the worst sister. Ever. She thinks she clearly failed Rebecca in some way. And that, until now, she avoided me entirely too much. I haven't found a way to tell her that I admired her for being both distant and polite. And that I had avoided her too.

"She doesn't owe me a thing," I told Raphael.

"Well, she's more used to my doing things for her," he added. "Don't worry, Leila. This is easy for me. And a pleasure."

Raphael is thoughtful in a way that the words *completely* and *totally* fail to describe. His thoughtfulness is *thorough* (a word with a spelling I always have to double-check and will never trust). I wonder if Clare ever thinks about what she does, in fact, owe him. More than I owe him for pointing out how a play about a suicide isn't going to inspire me to build its sets.

In early March, during Clare's third or fourth business trip, I finally ask Raphael if he's one of the people Rebecca saw during the weeks before she did it.

"I'm not sure," he says. "We had lunch, but that wasn't so unusual."

I tell him how I wasn't one of the people, but that she did say goodbye. I give him a version of seeing her through a window at Acca without mentioning anything about how I will one day sit in a café with a book I like and, possibly, a great love.

"So I sort of saw her," I say. "Maybe she meant for me to think that."

"That's probably right," Raphael says. "And in a way it's nicer not being one of the people she saw . . . before she did it."

"How's it nicer?" I ask him.

"You're one of the people she couldn't bring herself to say goodbye to," he says.

This is, as usual, really sweet of Raphael. But totally unbelievable. Rebecca took time to have lunch with him and he's surely someone it was hard for her to see one last time. Harder than seeing me would have been. Unless he's right and they had lunch because they often did. Not because she had to see him one last time.

If I knew who that was at Acca with her, I'd know something more. I'm not sure what exactly, but I'm certain it's important. Not necessarily the reason behind her death, but part of it.

"Why do you think she did it?" I ask Raphael. "I mean, do you know her reason?"

He's quiet for a while. I'm supposed to be doing homework and he's made a fire in the living room to make it less unpleasant. The deal at his house is I do homework for two hours and then I can watch half an hour of television. At home, I'm not allowed to watch at all—my mother believes TV will make me flunk out of school. Having a television, along with the equally forbidden Instant Messaging, has never seemed worth the argument.

Clare has a small TV that she uses to watch the news and, also, movies when she can't sleep. I do watch at friends' houses, of course, but the half-hour of anything I want on Raphael's wide, thin TV is still a thrill for me. As I flip through my math notes, I hope I haven't asked him something he doesn't want to think about.

"It would be nice if she'd had a specific reason," Raphael says. "Because otherwise one of us missed a chance to see that she was slipping away."

"Da and Clare act like her killing herself was in her personality or something."

"They're not wrong," Raphael says. "But what makes this time hard is how well she hid what she was doing."

What makes this time hard is that it worked. She died.

"She hid it all," he says. "And yet everything was there for us to see after the fact."

"What was there?" I ask.

Did he get a note I don't know about?

"She met with her lawyer, closed an account at the bank, and saw a lot of people," Raphael says. "But we didn't know how all the pieces would add up."

Rebecca's plan. The thing we all examine and stare at like a piece of modern art. What does it mean? What on earth does it mean? This is not a fun question outside of a museum.

"But who makes a plan without a reason?" I ask.

"I don't know," he says.

"There has to have been a reason. A good reason," I say. "And we're not seeing it. The way we didn't see obvious signs of her plan."

"Maybe," he says.

I suppose I was hoping Raphael would have an idea about how to start discovering Rebecca's reason. Or that he would know something I couldn't begin to guess. I go back to math, wishing for the umpteenth time that algebra didn't involve quite so many word problems. It's worse than physics.

When my two hours are up, Raphael puts down the journal he's been reading and asks, "What's your pick tonight?"

I like repeats of old black-and-white TV shows and Raphael likes a fake news show, but I don't get half of what makes it funny.

"You can decide," I say.

"Leila, about signs," he says. "And why Rebecca did it."

He pauses as if to consider what he wants to say.

"Often the very things we think of as signs are simply the things that we wish were true."

"And that makes them fake?" I ask.

"No, because what we wish for is real," he says. "But what they lead us to is, at best, unreliable."

"And at worst?"

He smiles. "That probably depends on what we're wishing for."

Based on what I can tell, Raphael's wish isn't, as family rumor says, to love my sister. It's to keep Clare safe from any and all harm. His desire to protect her is almost something you can touch. I wonder what unreliable things he sees, and how he knows which ones to trust.

If I want to uncover Rebecca's hidden story, then I need to follow the signs she's left. The unreliable as well as the true. I'll start with the man I saw when my sister was still alive. He's also been left behind and could possibly be a sign. If he's a fake one, at least it's a place to begin.

Ten

REBECCA KEPT A DATEBOOK, which now sits on her desk, next to her laptop. She called it *my boss*. In it was her schedule, reminder notes, and lists. It's my initial idea to go through this book, looking for the name of the man I last saw my sister with.

Da and Clare (and probably the police) have been all over Rebecca's computer and file cabinets. And they used her address book, which Rebecca had had since college, to notify friends. If they went through her datebook, it wouldn't have been because they were looking for this man whose name I don't know.

Other than information I don't have, I'm not sure what I'm looking for. But I'm convinced I'll know it when it finds me. I open the datebook and flip immediately to October. I see my tutor on Tuesdays and Thursdays. I'm looking for a day late enough in

October for it to have been dark by five.

I scan through the Tuesdays and Thursdays, and bang, there it is. October 23. In Rebecca's small, square-shaped handwriting: *Order #7874 pick up. Eyebrows. Check flour stats. 4:00 w/ T. Caffe Acca. Lettuce for C.*

T. That's not overly helpful. I pick up Rebecca's address book and almost scream when some pages fall out from the ancient binding. The book's not well organized—Raphael, for example, is under *C* (for *cousin*?)—and there are thirty-one people in the *T* section. Even if I knew what to say, I don't think I could place thirty-one phone calls to strangers. I put the date-book and address book back in their places. Then I sit on Rebecca's bed, asking whatever is left of her to forgive me for trespassing. And to let me know, if she can, how to find T.

I've been putting off quitting the tech crew. It will upset my parents, especially if I have to explain how I've reduced *The Children's Hour,* a play considered a political masterpiece (I've looked it up; this is the agreed-on opinion), to a reminder of Rebecca's death. Not to mention, how will it look to colleges?

How I will look to colleges is a question that has been stalking me since the end of tenth grade. Except that I need another four years to figure out what it is I want to do in the theater, I don't care about college so much. It matters a lot to my father, though. I only hope that the college I wind up liking is a place he thinks is good. Clare's college—a small, ruthlessly competitive place in Pennsylvania that made Da very proud of her—is not an option for me.

"No one expects you to go there," Clare says.

"Maybe no one expects it," I say. "But Da would love it if I got in."

"I wouldn't love it," she says. "I was hideously miserable there."

This is Clare's favorite thing to say about herself. Hideously miserable in college. Loved law school, but hideously miserable during her two years at the law firm. Madly in love with Elias (the *vile example of humanity* she lived with) until the last eight months of their relationship. Hideously miserable until Gyula found her. And, then, *Oh, joy.*

While *hideously miserable* is pretty easy to figure out, Clare means different things when she says *Oh, joy.* Ben, who spends just enough time with us to notice certain details, thinks it's always the opposite. That Clare means *What misery.* But I think it's more along the lines of Janie's comment about being blonde: joy's not all it's cracked up to be.

"How about a job?" Clare asks when I explain the trouble I'm having quitting the tech crew.

She'd been in complete agreement with Raphael that it was the wrong time for me to work on this play.

"A job," I say, trying to picture it. "I guess."

"I mean a fun job. One you'd like instead of one that will look good."

"What about Da?" I ask.

"I don't think he knows a lot of fun jobs," Clare says. "God, one year, he got Rebecca and me jobs in the hospital's processing department. I've never willingly filed since."

So it's lucky she has both a secretary and a research assistant.

"No, what do I tell Da," I say. "About quitting."

"You could *not* tell him," she says. "Although that might make it seem like we're hiding something."

Clare taps her glasses with her pen, a habit that can make Gyula grab her wrist. He says her eyes are the best way he has of guessing her thoughts. *So, please, do not have the risk to poke them out.*

"Without your eyes," he said, "I will not know that you are happy to see me."

Clare considered Gyula and I saw what he meant.

Her face had a composed, neutral look, but there was, behind seemingly calm eyes, a building laugh.

"You're always free to ask," Clare said.

"She's happy," I said, before remembering that Raphael had called my sister's life with Gyula complicated. I should probably stay out of it.

"Yes, it is so," Gyula said. "I know, but I like to see it."

And then Clare did smile at him and I wondered why Rebecca hadn't liked him. Watching Clare and Gyula was like seeing a man who didn't know quite what to do with his most treasured possession. Together they reminded me of a chandelier. One where the crystals and silver are so intricately arranged that you think *pretty* but also, *how is that possible*.

My sister stops her forbidden glasses-tapping and says to me,

"You get a job first, a fun job, and then we'll tell Da."

Tell him after the fact. He can't worry or object. Pretty clever.

"A fun job," I repeat and then, not very seriously, ask, "Can I go to work for a construction crew?"

"No, union rules are a nightmare in the city," says my ever practical sister, the lawyer. "Why don't you call your boss from last summer? The restaurant manager. Rebecca said they loved you there."

I got my job at Gaveston's last summer because Rebecca knew the owner. My sister made me work for her at the store before she would vouch for me. She wanted to make sure I could take an order, be polite to strangers, and handle a cash flow.

"She told you that I worked at Gaveston's?" I ask.

"She talked about you," Clare says. "It's only me who was the bad sister."

"That's not true," I say, finally contradicting this belief of hers. "I never thought of it like that."

"The famous big heart," Clare says, smiling. "Make your call, and if that doesn't pan out, I'll see what I can turn up."

I call my old boss, who says there's no room on the schedule for part-time help, but that a friend of his at Caffe Acca ("Downtown, on one of those tiny streets, do you know it?") is looking for someone to cover split shifts.

"It's what he gets for hiring actors," Greg says. "Professionals and students, I told him. It's the only way to go. Have him call me and I'll sing you to the heavens."

"Thanks," I say, in a fog of disbelief and shock.

Here's a big red flag that even I can see. If I get this

job, I could find T. Maybe he lives nearby. Maybe he always has coffee at Acca. Maybe if I worked there, I'd see him when he comes in. Bring his order *and* ask him who he was to my sister.

I arrange for an interview.

Hal Kranem, who is the kind of skinny that makes you think of a chain smoker, has three questions mostly relating to my schedule. Yes, I could do the four-to-seven split, three days a week. Yes, if I had to I could stay later. Yes, if he needs me, I could come in an hour late on the two days I get tutored. Rebecca once said that working in a restaurant is like joining a religion: total submission goes far toward gaining glory. Yes, I tell Hal, I do know Caffe Acca will lose its liquor license if a minor is caught serving drinks.

"I can take the order," I say. "But I can't bring it to the table."

"Or clear it," he says.

That's new, I think, hoping I'll be able to keep a regular coffee cup straight from an Irish coffee one.

"Or clear it," I say.

"Greg loved you," Hal says. "When can you start?"

I leave his small office almost convinced that my sister is still alive and working to shape my life. It's silly, I know, because I clearly owe this job to Greg, but I owed working for him to Rebecca. Maybe this is what people mean when they talk about feeling a hand touch them from beyond the grave.

Ben's not too happy with my sudden departure from the tech crew. He wants to know if it's because of him. More specifically, some other him.

"Are you dating somebody?"

I can't believe he's serious, but he is. The amount of time we spend together, which seems like a lot to me, seems like *hardly ever* to Ben.

"No, of course not," I say. "No."

My inability to work on this play feels private. While Ben used to be the first person who heard what was important and/or private, he isn't anymore. No matter how much I might wish otherwise. My living with Clare and Raphael, who are also consumed with Rebecca's memory, has made it impossible to even pretend that things are the same.

I miss Ben the way I miss my parents—as if I am the one who has gone on a trip. Not to an actual place, obviously, but to my version of what Clare calls *the new now*. She says it started for her when she landed at JFK, seventeen hours after Da's call to Budapest. She thinks it's the place you go to after the shock of Before and After wears off.

"You're my best friend," I say to Ben, wondering if that's still true.

If I've told a lie, I'll find a way to make it up to him. It's important to me that I never make him feel bad.

Eleven

I WRITE DA A LONG LETTER telling him about Acca and how when I'm not working, I'm doing "lots and lots" of homework. This is not a lie, and in fact, the school part of school has improved dramatically since Raphael appointed himself my full-time homework assistant. This makes exactly the kind of difference that experience has taught me it will. Up until eighth grade (a stretch of time I think of as B.T., for Before Tutor), I dreaded every second of school, with its dark, confusing cloud of information. Now I tend to think of the information as falling into two categories: hard and impossible.

In spite of Raphael's best efforts, English (but not math) has morphed from hard to impossible. We've been reading books and short stories by F. Scott Fitzgerald. Originally we were supposed to read Tolstoy and Chekhov, which I thought would be great because

I've already read the Chekhov plays. But the teacher changed the entire plan after the city was attacked.

"I think we need to look at something purely beautiful," she told us. "There's despair here, make no mistake, but beauty is his main aim."

Ben thinks she's going to get fired because she didn't ask Mr. Nordman, our headmaster, for permission to change the books. I've heard other students complain that she overuses words like *beauty* and *despair*. I like her because I always know what she's talking about. And, I like Fitzgerald.

Before January, we'd read one novel and a ton of short stories. They're all kind of the same. People are rich. People are beautiful. They're frequently cruel. And they always lose the one thing that's most important to them. Often a blonde girl is the precious thing that gets lost. How could any blonde girl on the planet not like this kind of stuff?

My tutor says I'm needlessly simplifying Fitzgerald's work and not reading it properly. Maybe so, but I like it. The stories are, if unhappy, also yummy. So it's a shock to discover that I can't understand the second book, which we started reading at the end of January.

It's doubly humiliating because I am about a hundred pages in before I realize that I don't know what the book is about. Ben says not to worry, that the book is boring, who cares what it's about. The thing is, the book *isn't* boring. It's something else entirely. Something I don't get, which is misery inducing. My tutor, however, is happy to hear it.

"Now we're finally reading," she says, and comes up with a plan of action.

I'm to read the book twice. Once to have read it and then again to have understood it. I don't know that it's working other than to make me feel like I have two part-time jobs. One waiting on the small round tables at Caffe Acca, and one reading *Tender Is the Night*.

When my shift at Acca is extra slow, Hal lets me stand in the back and read. I put my book up against the wall next to the pay phone and mark every passage that I think is important. My book is littered with pencil marks, which can't be right. Not everything can be important. I'm beginning to suspect that what matters is what happens *between* the events which are written down. Happens offstage, if you can say that about a book the way you do a play.

The story also goes backwards in time and then forwards again, which does not help my inept dyslexic self. I'm very close to deciding that people are like theater sets, some designed for certain things but not for others. It's as if I'm interested in stories more than I'm designed to *read* them. Perhaps they have to be attached to a real person in order for my brain to work.

For example.

There's a man who comes into Acca every Monday and Wednesday. He always orders chocolate raspberry cake and rarely eats any of it. He usually gets a coffee as well and drinks all of that. Black, one sugar. Like Raphael, but not Clare, who says putting sugar into coffee is a crime.

I've cleared away five practically untouched pieces of cake before I start paying close attention to him. As if other facts will explain what the deal is with the cake. Or, more specifically, what his story is. On his middle finger he wears a ring with raised hieroglyphic markings. Right hand, not left, which of course gives me fits to figure out. I can't decide how old he is—much younger than Gyula and who knows what in relation to Rebecca's T., who I'm still hoping will walk in one afternoon.

He sometimes reads the front section of the paper by folding the pages in half, lengthwise. Mostly though, he studies whatever is in a black binder he carries tucked up under his arm. He keeps a pen and small white pad in his jacket pocket and often makes notes about what he's reading.

It's a Monday when he sits at one of the tables in the window. Not the one Rebecca was at when I last saw her, but I still take it as a sign of some sort and bring his cake before he's asked for it. Up until then, I've always approached him as if I'm really wondering what he'll order.

I put the plate down, asking, "Do you want coffee today or iced tea?"

These are his two usual choices, and he looks up from his perfectly folded paper with a smile.

"Does this mean I'm predictable?" he asks.

"It means you know what you like," I say.

He leans back in his chair so that he doesn't have to look up at me so much. I tend to tower over everyone sitting down.

"You're right, I do," he says, and something about the way he's looking at me makes my blush start its spread up toward my scalp. What's wrong with me? I smile, hoping he won't notice the change in color.

"Coffee today?" I ask, firmly putting blushing and other unprofessional topics out of mind.

"That would be great," he says. "Thank you."

There are water glasses to be filled and orders to be

placed and tables to be wiped and people who need things and very quickly, just as my tables are emptying into the lull between coffee and dinner, I'm bringing him his change. After giving me a smile that doesn't quite meet my eyes, he's gone.

I bring his cake again on Wednesday, determined to withstand however he looks at me. He puts his hand against his heart and says,

"You remembered."

I laugh because he looks at once sweet and silly with his head cocked to one side and his hand like that.

"It's not a job that requires much," I say.

"Just a certain charming intelligence," he says.

And there goes my face—up in flames—but this time I know why. He's flirting with me, which would be a lot nicer without the blushing. By the time I get his coffee, I've stopped being such a twelve-year-old.

"So," he says, when I put his cup on the table. "May I ask your name?"

"It's Leila," I say. "Leila Abranel."

I love my last name. It has an elegance that *Leila* by itself can never attain. He looks suitably impressed, and although it's pretty quiet today, I'm away from his table until I bring the check.

"Leila means 'dark as night,'" he says. "Right?"

"Yes," I say. "No one ever knows that."

"It doesn't really fit you."

I'm never telling him my middle name. Nothing sounds less fitting than Gwendolyn. But I always thought Leila was a good name. For me. And then I see myself as if in a photograph with the caption *Dark as night.*

"Oh, you mean because of the blonde," I say. "But my personality is dark. Very dark."

"I'm not sure I'd believe that," he says.

"Don't let the smile fool you," I say, amazed at myself.

I'm just flirting away here. Dial it down, Leila. He's not that good-looking. And it's more the attention I like than him, which is rude of me. I pull myself into the how-do-you-do expression I use when meeting friends of my parents.

"My cheerfulness is a façade," I say, glad to have found a place for one of my SAT vocabulary words.

"No, it's not the smile," he says. "It's . . . no, you're translucent."

He's in luck that this is a frequent adjective from *Tender Is the Night.* I've had to look it up and figure out that in the book, when a person or an event is described as translucent, it isn't a good or a bad thing. It's more that the someone or thing is important. Prized and rare. This is quite possibly the nicest compliment I've ever gotten, even if he doesn't mean exactly what the book does.

"Thank you," I say. "That's lovely."

He just looks at me.

"Anyway, my name's Leila," I add. "Even if it doesn't fit."

"Eamon," he says, standing up and holding out his hand. "Eamon Greyhalle. It's very nice to meet you, Leila."

I shake his hand and take my tray to the kitchen, ignoring the zing-zang-zoom which his skin sent shooting up and across my body. That I did not expect, as I've been shaking hands since forever. Until I was thirteen, I had to shake hands and curtsey with everyone I met. My sisters had had to do this too and always thought it was ridiculous.

I didn't mind it except for when people would look at Da and say, *Oh, my, can you make her do that again?* As hard as it is to meet strangers, I've always felt protected by my knowing how to do it. You look someone straight in the eye, hold their hand with a firmness that doesn't threaten to break it, and you smile.

There's no zing-zang-zooming involved. I'm pretty sure that's against the how-to-meet-someone rules.

When I tell Ben, Clare, and Raphael about Acca, I leave Eamon out entirely. Instead I focus on how the job is easy and fun. I am, as I knew I would be, really good at it. In more ways than I care to count, I tell them, I'm the perfect waitress.

"It's because you treat people well," Raphael says. "You've always been like that."

"You're perfect at a lot of things," Clare says, which is nice.

"You're lucky you haven't dropped anything yet," Ben says, which is funny because I once dropped a cup of soup in his lap and all he said, very quietly, was *Hey. Ow.*

A few days after we shake hands, Eamon asks about *Tender Is the Night.*

"So you're always reading by the phone," he says. "What has such a hold on you?"

"You've seen me do that?" I ask. "I'm only allowed to do that when no one needs anything."

"Well, sometimes I look for you when I don't need anything."

And we're back to flirting. I like how conversations with Eamon veer around from the normal to the silly.

"It's a book I'm reading twice," I say.

"What book is that good?" he asks.

"I'm not sure it's good," I say.

"And so you're reading it twice because?"

He has a way of making me believe that everything I say, from *Coffee?* to *I'm reading,* is of great interest to him. When I worked for Rebecca last summer, she told me that the reason flirting was fun was that no one meant anything by it. So maybe Eamon is not really interested in what I say, but I go ahead and tell him how the book happens off the page. How I really liked that he called me *translucent* because of the book. How I wish the story made more sense to me.

"I read it in college too," Eamon says. "But I don't remember if it made sense. I'll have to go back and look."

I want to ask him what he's reading in that binder, what the notes are for. What's written on the ring and why he comes here. But I'm a waitress. And I'm not exactly sure how much one can ask a strange man about himself. About anything. No matter how polite he is or how nice his hands look holding his coffee cup.

Twelve

WHAT'S IMPORTANT IN ALL THIS, what makes me attach Eamon to my story, happens the next week or the one right after. He isn't at Acca that Monday, which I don't realize until Wednesday when I see him sit down in the café's other section. I smile hello and then turn my attention to two women trying to decide between an éclair and a napoleon. I gather they're going to split it. They ask which I prefer and I say,

"Maybe I can ask the kitchen for a plate with half of each."

I feel a tap on my back. It's Drew, who works the shift with me.

"The guy at table nine wants you," he says.

"That's a perfect solution," one of the women says to me. "Do we have to pay for both?"

"I'll be right there," I tell Drew and say to the woman, "I'll ask."

"We could take the other halves home," the other woman says. "Maybe Mama would like them."

"She does love them," the first woman says.

Sisters! Who call their mother Mama, just like Clare and Rebecca. I want to ask them a thousand things and warn them to stay alive, but there are some things even I know cannot be said. To anyone.

"Can we do that?" they ask together and then start laughing.

"I'm sure you can," I say. "I'll bring it right out."

I pause at table nine and ask Eamon if he needs anything.

"I'm in the wrong section, aren't I, bunny?"

He calls me that sometimes, and when I asked him if he thought I looked like a rabbit, he said, *No, you look young and worth protecting.*

"You're in Drew's section," I answer. "He's great with cake and coffee."

"How much commotion if I move?" Eamon asks.

Hal's looking right at me, and no wonder. I'm not doing my job.

"The customer is king," I say. "But maybe order something else so there's a reason I'm standing here."

Eamon asks for a glass of wine and off I go, passing Drew arriving with the chocolate raspberry cake. I check with Hal that it's okay to tell the kitchen to cut pastries in half and then ask him to bring a Merlot over to the man at table nine.

"The one who's moving?" Hal asks.

"That's right," I say, without turning around.

"Is he bothering you?" Hal asks me.

"No," I say. "No. He's really nice."

"Just remember that some people think waitresses are available," Hal says. "Like what's on the menu."

"Yuck," I tell him and get back to work.

The sisters act like seven-year-olds over their dessert. They're so happy to be eating it. When I give them the boxed-up remains I tell them both that I hope their mother likes it.

"Just my mother," says the woman taking the box. "We're not sisters."

So you never know. Raphael is right. A lot of the things we see are what we wish.

"I've read your book," Eamon says when I come to clear his table. "It took longer than I thought."

"You did?" I ask, almost dropping my little tray of dishes. "A week's not long."

"Well, I was sorry not to see you Monday," he says. "But I thought I should finish."

I put his bill down and say I'll be right back. I clear

the rest of my tables so I can focus on what he has to say about *Tender Is the Night.* I can't believe he read it. Even Raphael hasn't done that. He just keeps saying he has every faith in my abilities. That's a mistake.

"So, what's it about?" I ask, hoping this isn't cheating.

I'm still going to keep on reading it twice, but it'd be nice to know.

"I think it's about disappointment," Eamon says. "Life has failed everyone in this book. Everything they touch leads them to ruin."

"Ruin," I say, thinking, of course, about Janie and Julian, but also about Rebecca.

She wasn't part of a ruined great love, but . . . she was obviously disappointed. Even before she killed herself, I knew as much as that.

"I make and sell cake," she used to say whenever you asked about her work. "It is what it is."

When she was a hospice nurse, she said, "I watch people die."

Rebecca said *It is what it is* more than Clare says *Oh, joy.* Did life fail my sister? Did she think that?

And then a thousand things about *Tender Is the Night* snap into place. Failure and disappointment. That makes sense. Maybe Rebecca, like the people in the book, felt them too much.

No one ever believed you were a failure. But, of course, it's too late to tell her. And it's not what I would have told her if I'd known her plan. I try not to get lost in Rebecca World and bring my mind back to the living.

"You must think I'm so dumb," I say to Eamon. "That only took you a week."

"I think you're what, twenty-two? Twenty-four?" Eamon asks. "A book about life's disappointments is a bad fit for you. That's all."

I wonder how come I'm the only one in my class who can't understand it. It would be nice to think I'm too young instead of too dyslexic. And then: he thinks I'm over twenty? For a while now, people have assumed I'm older. I think it's the height and the whole needing an underwire bra. But Rebecca says it's because Da's never stopped expecting me to be older.

"It's as if you seem older because of how he treats you," she says. "And the height helps."

She said. Remember, Leila, Rebecca is dead.

Twenty-two? Well, that makes up for being too dumb to know what I'm reading. Or does that make me more dumb?

"I'll be twenty soon," I say.

Twenty actually feels as far away as Poland, but my parents are always talking about how time flies and maybe it does for Eamon as well, whose age remains a mystery.

"You're not twenty yet?" he asks. "Oh, shoot me. When's your birthday?"

"June," I say. "Why?"

"We can talk about that in June," he says.

"June's ages away," I say, thinking, *Talk about what?*

"It'll keep," he says. "I hope I didn't sound too ridiculous just now, talking about the book."

"No, no. It was really nice of you," I say. "To take the time and all. It was nice."

I have the worst vocabulary. You're so *nice.*

"Well, thanks. It's that, you know, my father can really get long-winded," Eamon says. "I'm terrified of turning into him."

"Mine's like that," I say. "But you were helpful. I mean, I'd missed the whole failure thing."

The whole failure thing? Have I lost my mind? I remember how in ninth grade Da charged me twenty dollars every time he heard me use the word *like* as if it were the verb "to say." I owed him a hundred and eighty dollars by the end of three days, but I stopped saying it so much and Da stopped complaining that it pained him to hear me speak.

I was totally relieved when I gave him some babysitting money and he said I could consider my debt canceled. But right this second I wish he'd thought to charge me for sounding as if I were a moron. Why couldn't I have said, *You were of great assistance. I hadn't grasped the novel's many nuances.*

Of course, now I think of it. But Eamon doesn't look as if I sounded especially moronic.

"I don't think you missed it so much as it didn't jump out," he says. "And maybe I've missed what it's really about."

"Oh, no," I say, thinking carefully. "Failure does resonate throughout the book."

He smiles, saying, "I'll see you next week, Leila."

"Bye, Eamon."

And while saying his name feels like a prized and rare occurrence, for many months what I remember about that day—what I write down—is that Rebecca's reason might be related to some kind of big disappointment that we haven't uncovered. Am I looking for one big disappointment? Or were there a lot of little ones that became, all at once, too big? Or will the secret I find be a failure? In the end, what will it matter, as neither of those things can have killed her.

After all, I always thought that Janie and Julian's great love was ruined because it ended. I never thought there was a secret failure to it. The story I tell myself is of a big, consuming love which produced my sisters, but could not continue. A great love ending was failure and disappointment enough.

But as Da and Janie proved, it was nothing to die over. Instead, it made Janie work more than usual and Da listen to sad music. So what happened to my sister? In my notebook, I write down the date and what Eamon told me. I underline the word *ruin* and put a question mark after Rebecca's name.

And another one after the word *June.*

Thirteen

FOR CLARE'S BIRTHDAY, which is the last Friday in April, Raphael has helped me to make a cabinet. I didn't need the help as much as he thought, but I was glad to have it while drilling mortises. My mother had shown me how, but a good three years ago. In this way, I didn't mess up and Raphael got to feel useful, which is pretty much what he lives for.

We designed the cabinet to fit between the living room windows and to hold pillows and blankets. A kind of portable linen closet.

"It's beautiful," Clare says. "Oh, and we can put these on the top."

Raphael has given her white lilies in a vase made of heavy blue glass. It's from the same German glassware company that Clare negotiated with when she started working for Edward Schweitzer. He's her boss who owns all the hotels.

"That was ages ago," Clare says. "How on earth did you remember?"

"You had quite a lot to say," Raphael tells her. "About the glasses used in hotel bars."

I wish I had been there to hear my sister holding forth on which glasses hotels have and why. Last month, I went to dinner with Clare and Gyula at the hotel where he stays. When I said I didn't want to order eight-dollar orange juice, they both made a list of all the nice details in the hotel's restaurant. The waiters' jackets, the red wallpaper, the dark tables, and how my water glass sat on a ribbed coaster.

"All of it is the result of contracts," Clare told me.

"Contracts designed to create a refuge for people," Gyula added. "Charge anything less for juice and nothing gets reupholstered, the jackets lose their shape, and —"

"Slowly but surely everything falls apart," Clare finished for him.

It was definitely one of the best nights of my life. I knew I'd never go into a restaurant or a hotel or a bar without thinking of Clare and Gyula's lesson on contracts and prices.

"I was so happy when that deal came through," she says now, holding the vase up for inspection. "Edward was very impressed. He thought I'd never get the price down, but I'd researched it to death."

It's becoming possible to imagine Clare happy. You can see it in bits. Like when she's with Gyula or had a good day at work or spent time with Raphael. I wouldn't say she's totally happy now, but for the past couple of weeks she hasn't been crying in the bathroom. She told me that on her last business trip, something had shifted. Or cracked.

"I've started noticing things again," she said. "The way certain kinds of soap come wrapped in tissue paper. The shape of espresso cups. Dried flowers in bowls. You know, stupid little things that shouldn't matter, but that I like."

I thought that maybe her brain had been foggy too (not in the same way as mine, but in a Clare-ish way) and that because she's smarter than I am, she'd been able to shake it off. I loved her for finding her way back to soap and cups.

She puts the vase on the shelves and steps back a little.

"It's all so perfect," she says, putting her hand on my shoulder and looking at Raphael. "So we're still on for tomorrow?"

"Yes," he says. "Of course."

We're going ice-skating. There's an indoor place called Sky Rink down at the Chelsea Piers. When Clare and Rebecca had figure-skating lessons, Sky Rink was still in midtown. *Decades ago,* as Clare said. *I was little then.* She's going out with Gyula tonight. He was in Toronto this week and found a way to get here for the day, but he has to go back to Canada first thing in the morning.

I hand Clare the earrings Gyula sent when he still thought he was going to miss her birthday. They're little pearls arranged around a diamond in a gold mesh setting. When Clare opened the box, she simply stared at them before finally saying,

"How odd."

"They're beautiful," I said. "God, they're like . . . beautiful."

At least I know I'm not articulate. *Beautiful* is as bad as *nice.* I've got to learn not to sound so . . . limited.

"They're exquisite," Clare said, picking one up. "It's just Mama always told us you never accept jewelry from a man you've no plans to marry."

This is exactly the kind of information my mother would never give me. There's a rule about men and marriage and jewelry other than the engagement ring? Well, now I know. And it sounds more important than Janie's what-to-order-on-a-date rule.

"I've told Gyula that," Clare said. "He wanted to give me a necklace a year after we met."

"What did he say?" I asked her, guessing that Gyula isn't that much fun when he doesn't get his way.

"He said he wasn't giving it to my mother, and then he was truly offended when I wouldn't take it," Clare said, with a buried laugh. "Not one of my more shining moments."

"Do you think the earrings mean he wants to marry you?"

I sort of hoped they did, which was disloyal to Raphael, but I thought there was something in Gyula—something hard and glittery and far away—that suited Clare. You could tell that Gyula, unlike Raphael, didn't long to protect her; he assumed he already did. And I thought she was sparkly around him. When together, they didn't just remind me of how a chandelier was arranged, but of how it gleamed.

"No, the earrings do not mean that," Clare said. "Believe me."

She opened the card and translated from the German, which is what she and Gyula speak when he doesn't trust his English. *So glad you were born. Please allow them. Yours, etc., G.*

I said that I thought this was the best love note I'd ever heard, and she smiled, saying, "Yes, he does these very well."

At the time, this did not sound like a ringing endorsement, but tonight, wearing them, she looks like sparkly, happy Clare in the earrings. And a dress she's pulled from the back of her closet. It's light green, zips up the side, has a square neckline and no sleeves.

"You're going to freeze," Raphael says. "Take a sweater or something."

"It used to have a matching jacket," Clare says. "But I lost it. Mama was furious."

So this is one of the Janie dresses. According to Rebecca, Janie had given them both *insanely beautiful clothes* to wear to opening nights of shows she had worked on. They were clothes to admire, Rebecca told me. Not to wear. And yet, here is Clare all decked out in one for her thirty-seventh birthday.

"You look beyond lovely," Raphael says, handing her a black raincoat from the closet.

"Not too old?" Clare asks.

When Da called, he told her she was now old enough to start lying about her age. A bit of information she could probably have done without. I know he was trying to make conversation, as Da usually says the worst things when he has no idea what to say.

"Certainly not," Raphael says.

The coat, while not matching, looks elegant. Have a good time, we say. See you tomorrow. Happy birthday.

In the kitchen, Raphael puts on water for pasta and I grate cheese.

"Did you see the earrings?" I ask, wanting to warn him in case the jewelry gift means what Clare says it does not.

"I did," he says. "My mother has a pair like them."

I try to picture Aunt Ingrid in Clare's earrings but can't. These earrings are their own unique pair. I can so easily see Gyula picking them out, his hand hovering over different pairs. I had even imagined the small, quiet store where jewelry is brought out from locked cases and displayed on velvet for selection.

"Just like them?" I ask.

"Maybe not exactly," Raphael says. "Pearls, gold, you know."

"These have diamonds," I say. If he doesn't want to be warned, fine.

"I hope it goes well tonight," Raphael says.

"Why won't it?" I ask.

What did I fail to notice? She looks good and is with Gyula. Can it go badly?

"It's only that this is the first time he's been with her on her birthday," Raphael says.

They've been going out for five years, so this does not reflect well on Gyula. What can he have been thinking? Even after the divorce, William would call Rebecca on her birthday.

"How come?" I ask.

"I suspect she always told him it wasn't important and he finally doesn't believe her," Raphael says. "It's also her first birthday without Rebecca."

So this is what's worrying him. Not Gyula or earrings, but Rebecca's absence. It's likely to make Clare miserable when Raphael wants her to be happy. My brain immediately jumps to August 30, which will be Rebecca's first birthday without Rebecca. That's going to be horrible. I remember that on Janie's birthday last year Da called both girls and was very quiet in a loud sort of way. Mom came home early and took him out to dinner even though it was her night to work late. It was smart of her, because when they came back he was more himself.

"Clare's doing better," I say to Raphael. "She's not crying as much in the bathroom."

"She still goes in there to cry?"

Well, how would I know from "still"? His old news is my fresh information.

"I think so," I say. "Yes."

"God, those girls," he says. "Abranel masterpieces."

In this instant, for the very first time, I see that I am not the only one who looks at my two sisters as one. A thing apart from who they are or were. That my sisters are also people makes them, to me, that much more interesting. That much more deserving of my attention and the stories I've given them.

"Gyula might help her forget," I say. "You know, that it's another day Rebecca has missed."

"He might," Raphael says. "He will. Let's get dinner on the table."

After we're done eating, I do the dishes and, in return, Raphael says we can skip math. Do I want to learn gin rummy? He and his father taught my sisters years ago.

"I know you and Ben play crazy eights," Raphael says. "Or is it 'played'? I'm not sure how much time you spend with him now."

"We still play," I say.

But only during lunch instead of for hours after school. On weekends, we sometimes used to deal my parents in even though we were pretty sure my mother cheated. I like the idea of playing cards with someone from here in *the new now*.

"Gin is a little different," Raphael says.

We sit at the table, playing with all the cards face-up, waiting until I get the hang of it enough to play for real. What we are really waiting for, of course, is sleep. Each evening of the past five months has ended with the hope that the next day will be easier. That it will finally be a day less heavily shaded by Rebecca.

Fourteen

CLARE COMES HOME A LITTLE AFTER TEN. And, as she's putting away coat and shoes, says she and Gyula have broken up. That she'd thought of checking herself into a hotel until she could pull herself together, but that that's the kind of thing Rebecca would do. So, instead, she's going to take a very long bath and go to bed. She's fine. Really.

"Can you tell us what happened?" Raphael asks, and I know he's trying to keep her out of the bathroom.

"I don't want to talk about it," she says. "I want to kill him."

"We don't have to talk," Raphael says. "We can sit and plan a murder. Leila, get your sister some tea."

"Water," Clare says. "Can I have some water?"

I bring her a bottle of water and a glass.

"Gyula's become an investor in the Vivfilli," she

says. "He heard I was researching it, thought I might like it, and bought into it. Oh, joy."

The Vivfilli is the name of the lost hotel in Barcelona.

"Researching it?" Raphael asks, somehow managing to get her to sit down by pushing a chair close to where she's standing.

"I have contacts in Spain," Clare says. "A law firm. They got me the Vivfilli's bank records. The renovation contracts."

"Yes, of course," Raphael says, indicating he knows what research means but his question is "Why?"

"I don't know," Clare says quietly. "When we were little, Rebecca and I used to play hotel owner the way normal girls played house."

She peels the blue and white label from the bottle and starts to shred it, saying,

"I must have wanted to be in touch with whatever's left of her. It's stupid, I know."

"It's not," I say. "Not at all."

I'm thinking of my job at Caffe Acca and of bringing Eamon cake because his table was close to where Rebecca once sat. Of all the fear and longing that goes into touching her things.

"He says"—here Clare's voice breaks, but she puts

her hands up like stay away signs—"he says I can have a job there now. That he can put me in charge of the renovations. Let me run the deal."

"You know he meant to show you he understands," Raphael says. "That's the only reason he bought the Vivfilli."

"Invested in it. He can't afford to buy it," Clare says. "If he could afford to buy it, it would make him happier than my moving to Budapest ever would."

"You're moving to Budapest?" I ask.

She's speaking so fast and there's too much to follow. Raphael defending Gyula, Clare almost crying somewhere other than the bathroom, a lost hotel becoming found, and . . . I can't keep track.

"I guess he thinks Barcelona is a compromise between Budapest and here," Clare says. "We've been talking for years about how one of us has to move."

"Years," Raphael says.

His voice is quiet, but he looks almost entertained at the idea of this endless talk that has obviously gone nowhere.

"Well, Gyula should be the one to move," I say. "You have a job here."

I'm not anxious for my remaining sister to pack

up for Budapest. Although, that seems unlikely if they've really broken up.

"I was never going to go," Clare says. "We knew he could never leave his business and I could never leave, oh, God, I could never leave while Mama and Rebecca were here."

And she's crying for real now. Enough to be unable to keep us away. I somewhat ineffectually pat her knees while she almost crawls up against Raphael, crying and crying and crying. *Shhhh,* he keeps saying. *Shhhh.* I like that he's not telling her it will be okay and that everything will look different in the morning—all things I've been told while crying.

Shhh. Shh. Until she quiets down and pulls away from him to snatch as much Kleenex from the box as she can.

"I'm so sorry," she says. "I should clearly have hit a hotel."

"And let us miss this?" Raphael asks lightly. "Leila and I were just sitting here saying, I hope Clare comes home and falls apart because it's been such a long time since we've had anything to do."

It gets her laughing, and she wipes her eyes with the backs of her hands, saying,

"I probably cried mascara into my contacts."

"At least it didn't run down your face," Raphael says.

"I don't even want to think about all the creepy ways he could have found out I was researching the Vivfilli," Clare says.

"Maybe he knows your lawyer in Spain," Raphael says.

It sounds better than the idea of Gyula checking up on her. Or spying or whatever other creepy ways Clare has in mind.

"On top of everything else, he told me I shouldn't make a major decision like this until Rebecca had been dead a year."

We're all quiet. I'd have thought Gyula would know better than to try to prevent Clare from breaking up with him by reminding her of Rebecca's death.

"As if it's because of her that I've had it," my sister says. "He thinks a hotel will fix everything? Or a job?"

Fix what? What was broken *before* they broke up?

Clare stands up and laughs in a high, nervy way, saying, "I thought I was going to throw something at him."

She stalks off and I guess Raphael thinks it's safe to let her have her long bath. He looks kind of wrecked. I pick up Clare's discarded tissues and ask if he wants some tea.

"I think I need a drink," he says.

"They don't have anything," I tell him.

I still think of the kitchen as belonging to both of my sisters. They have flour, two kinds of salt, tea, coffee, and bottled water. They don't have alcohol.

"Rebecca kept Scotch behind the good plates," he says, following me to the kitchen and locating the bottle.

I watch him pour it, take a sip, put ice in it, and take another sip before pouring the whole thing down the drain.

"That never does what it's supposed to," he says.

My mother sometimes has wine at dinner. Rebecca always did. I knew Janie drank brandy at the end of the workday and, on occasion, to sleep. Da likes vodka on ice, but only every now and then. Does Gyula drink? I can't remember. He probably is tonight. Before she started crying, I kept waiting for Clare to reveal his true crime. He invested in a hotel she loves to distraction. Is that so awful?

"I don't understand," I say. "What did Gyula do?"

"I think it's more what he hasn't done," Raphael says.

I wait because that's not a good enough answer.

"I suppose Clare has always suspected him of trying to buy her," Raphael says. "When what she wants is for him to love her."

"He does love her," I say. "Of course he loves her."

"Maybe it's not enough."

I feel that familiar dark cloud descending as I struggle to make sense of what has happened. Who buys a hotel—who invests in one—for someone he doesn't love enough? And what does it mean to buy someone? I'm pretty certain that Gyula's being rich is not something Clare dislikes.

But what if Janie's rule about accepting jewelry is really about money. Accepting money (even the kind disguised as jewelry) obligates you. It's not so different from my mother's notion that I should always split the check. Clare could like Gyula's money without ever wanting to owe him anything.

Perhaps Gyula needs for her to be in his debt. Even if I don't know where he's failed Clare, he must know. Thus the necklace, the earrings, the hotel. To cancel out the bad stuff.

"What matters is not what Gyula did," Raphael says. "But how Clare feels about it. This makes two people who haven't been there for her."

Who've left her.

"We're two people," I say. "We can fix her."

"We can try," he says.

Fifteen

TRYING TURNS OUT TO BE HARDER than we had anticipated. Gyula's not ready to let Clare make this last decision. He calls and calls and calls again before he flies back from Canada to see her. A gesture he ruins by pointing out how much work he's had to rearrange in order to do this. Clare, who left her own office early to meet him, was, she tells me, underwhelmed.

He thinks she's making a mistake. She thinks he doesn't know why she's upset.

"He'll die believing that investing in the Vivfilli was a brilliant idea," she says. "He says I've entirely missed the point."

Because I don't know what Gyula hoped the hotel would make up for, I don't say anything.

"And to make it worse," Clare says, "I miss him."

That I already knew. She cries when he calls and when he doesn't. She's terrified of winding up alone forever. More terrified of settling for someone not right for her. She does the crying over Gyula out in the living room. She even lets me sit on the end of her sofa bed and make her tea.

"Half the time, I think he's right," Clare says. "I've left him because of Rebecca."

"I thought it was because of the hotel," I say.

"He always thinks he knows everything," she says. "That he can fix it all."

So that was it. He tried to fix what had happened when Rebecca died and he did it in the wrong way. And Clare can't or won't forgive him. She can only cry and be mad. Or sad. Or whatever it is that has made being with Gyula worse than not being with him is.

"You could try being friends with him," I say, remembering her reaction when I'd told her that Ben and I weren't dating anymore.

"No," Clare says. "Gyula and I aren't friends who fell in love."

I think of how Clare worked to fit him into her schedule, how pleased she was when he sent flowers or phoned. I know she called him whenever she had trouble at work.

"But you are friends," I say. "Right?"

"Yes, but not . . . He likes to call me his most beloved problem," Clare says. "We're not friends so much as two people who have this love that doesn't work."

"How did you know that you loved him?" I ask. "If you weren't friends first?"

"It's like when you want to sleep with someone," Clare says. "You just know. So even if you're scared or think it's unwise, you know. Here he is. I love him."

She starts to cry again, but she is also swearing a little bit. And soon, she is laughing. As well as crying. I give her tissues and more tea.

In the days that follow, I listen when she wants to talk and sit when she wants company but no conversation. I imagine that my mother, far away in Poland, is doing much the same for Da. The difference would be that Mom already knows him and I am learning things about Clare and Gyula that I never thought to ask.

That they met on a construction site. That whenever he puts her on a plane home, he kisses both sides of her face and each of her fingers. That their favorite hotel is in Munich, but that the best trip they ever took was to Salzburg for five days of doing nothing. That she wishes he had liked Rebecca more. That he called Janie *formidable,* is slightly afraid of Da, and thinks I will grow up to be a beauty.

Mostly I find out that it's over. This is the one thing Clare says again and again. I don't ask how she knows. *You just know,* she said about loving someone. And then one day at dinner, he mentions a hotel and you no longer love him.

Until now, I hadn't realized that the whole boyfriend thing becomes harder as we get older. Not easier, as I had expected. After all, everything else has improved with practice.

It gets harder for the men, too, I think. Gyula must have his own version of Clare's fear and anger. Eventually, they both agree that a mental and physical distance is needed. Gyula asks her to agree to meet him after six months have passed. Some neutral place. She can pick the city. There shouldn't be any need for contact until then.

Just as all of this is unfolding and settling and blowing up, school is hurtling toward its end. I somehow muddle through English by working with my tutor on an essay about Fitzgerald and his descriptions of women. Though I don't go and see the production of *The Children's Hour,* I spend an hour with Ben admiring the sets. There's no bay window, which I would've built, but it all looks good.

I ask a million questions, as if I can't figure out for myself how the tech crew did this or that. Watching Clare and Gyula struggle to reach a civilized breakup has made me incredibly grateful to Ben and the way he has allowed us to move backwards. It's so weird. I *should* love him. Love him enough to know I want to sleep with him.

Maybe I'll know after the summer, when we've had our own mental and physical break. Which will start in a few weeks, after the yearbook is distributed, grades are posted, and I leave for Poland.

But only for ten days and not, as I had feared, for the whole summer. Mom is worried I'll mope around with nothing to do and then she'll have two moping people on her hands. She didn't put it that way, of course, but I could tell she was relieved when I said Clare had offered to find me an internship with one of Janie's friends.

"That's a wonderful idea," my mother said. "You loved Janie's work. And you read all those plays."

I know that Mom would partly like to have me there. To keep her company and to help with whatever it is Da might be needing. But I also know that most of her time and attention is taken up with helping my father get used to having only two daughters. As one of those remaining two, I'd be less than useful.

The job Clare finds for me is with Charlotte Strom, a theatrical producer who was a friend of Janie's.

"Does she light things?" Ben asks when I tell him of the job.

"No, I think she hires lighting designers," I say. "I'm not sure what she does exactly."

"It'll be cool," he says. "Now you can see what theater jobs are like."

Ben is going to spend the summer in Montana with his brother, who has gotten them both jobs at a summer camp for autistic children. Ben will be working in the computer lab. His brother is studying to be a social worker so it's a perfect place for him. They both know exactly what they'll be doing.

At some point during the summer, I hope I'll learn what *theatrical producer* means. During the brief interview which she called a formality, Charlotte told me that she'd have taken a bullet for Janie.

"Giving gainful employment to her ex-husband's daughter is my great pleasure."

There's no end of names for me. *Julian's back-up plan. Her ex-husband's daughter.* My sisters can't say they have as many labels. I'm supposed to call Mrs. Strom Charlotte, although she is mostly referred to as Mrs. Strom. In spite of never having been married.

"In the world of money, *Mrs.* has an authority *Ms.* never will," she said. "It's less threatening for people to think I started my career by using my husband's money."

I can't imagine either Janie or my mother ever approving of that, but maybe Charlotte has her reasons.

"We'll be busy," she said, putting out a cigarette she'd lit, but not smoked. "You'll see."

She told me there would be rehearsals for the new Isaac Rebinsehn play. And a miserable wreck of a revival to rethink, since she's already losing money on it.

"It'll be grand," she said. "Or a disaster."

I report all of this to Clare and Raphael. My sister says that of all of Janie's friends, Charlotte is the most overbearing, but that Da's probably trained me to handle that.

"I'd hardly call Julian overbearing in any real sense of the word," Raphael says.

From certain things Clare has mentioned about Uncle Harold, I'm guessing that the Abranels seem easygoing compared to the Barclays. The vague picture I had of Raphael's parents (a man who printed money married to a woman whose first husband was Da's brother) has come into sharper focus.

Uncle Harold owned a chain of drugstores. The reason everyone knew him in Paris was that he had sued a French bank over a bad loan. It was in all the papers. Aunt Ingrid was, even before Da's brother died, a nervous woman who let people do everything for her.

"I don't think my mother ever opened her own mail" was how Raphael put it.

Clare added that Aunt Ingrid was also heartbreakingly beautiful.

"She's still good-looking," Clare said. "But when we were little, you could watch her for hours. Rebecca and I thought anyone that perfect-looking must be a special effect."

I had the sense that if Aunt Ingrid never opened her own mail, it was because she never had to. Uncle Harold clearly ran her life, but it didn't sound like she minded. Raphael said his father treated Aunt Ingrid like he owned her and that, in a way, he did.

I'm happy to realize that if the Barclays, along with most of the Abranels, once seemed as distant as the lost hotels, that is no longer true.

Sixteen

THIS IS THE FIRST YEAR I'm not dreading exams. I'm not looking forward to them, of course, but I know where I'm weak and, for the most part, why. As much as someone like me can be, I'm prepared to write down what I know in return for a grade.

At work, I've improved enough at flirting so that talking to Eamon seems less a disturbing thrill and more something I enjoy and look forward to. During the final weeks of May, therefore, I'm fairly convinced that my biggest task ahead is finding a way to spend ten days in Poland without disrupting my parents' new, necessary life.

Eamon spent time in Warsaw (but not Krakow) a few years ago when he was *between jobs.* He normally lives in Los Angeles and writes for television shows. His father's sick and Eamon has moved back to the city to look after him. It's what Eamon is doing here twice a week; Mr. Greyhalle has physical therapy nearby and Caffe Acca has better coffee than the office waiting room.

Eamon's not between jobs now, though. He's been hired to turn an animated Japanese television show into a live-action American TV series. The black binder has all of the translated scripts and storyboards from the Japanese show. I know a lot more about the television stuff than I do about Mr. Greyhalle. Eamon doesn't like to talk about his father and I don't think his mother is a great conversation starter either.

But Poland is a safe topic. He says he's heard Krakow is a beautiful city, not destroyed by the war (which makes my head hurt until I work out which one: the Second World War). Although, he says, I'd like Budapest better. I should absolutely go to Budapest. A perfect way to spend my twentieth birthday. Kidnap my father for a weekend in Hungary.

I haven't mentioned Rebecca to Eamon, so he doesn't know what my parents are really doing. *Helping train medical staff* sounds a lot better than *fleeing suicide*. I have, for the most part, managed to keep Rebecca separate from my upcoming trip, my exams, and Clare's ongoing saga with Gyula.

The idea that Rebecca is involved in their breakup has made me frightened of looking at just how much my sister is still alive. I've been almost too successful at keeping Rebecca at a distance. Something I realize when, at long last, T. enters Caffe Acca.

I remember with blazing clarity why I took this job in the first place. How on earth had I forgotten? My time is not to be wasted on exams or jobs or talking to Eamon. My time's not even for deciphering Clare's misery. It's for following Rebecca's road up until the impossible end.

At first I don't recognize him. It's unusually busy, as if everyone is getting a jump on the upcoming holiday weekend by going out for cake and coffee. I've barely had time to smile at Eamon and hardly register that two men are sitting down at a table I haven't cleared yet. It's when I approach the table, seeing him in profile (the mirror image of my last look at him), that I realize who he is. It's worked. My plan has been a success.

Except.

There's no plan for after this moment. My entire plan has been to work here, see him when he comes in, and ask about Rebecca. Reasonable enough, but fairly vague on that last point. *How* to ask such a thing. My plan has failed to take into account the fact that I can't.

I mean, I can barely breathe. I wipe off the table. Ask what they'd like. T. wants an iced espresso and the other man orders a white wine spritzer, a salad, and the cheese plate.

I make the espresso drink while asking Hal to deal with the spritzer.

"You're white as a sheet," Hal says. "Do you need to sit down?"

"I'm not," I say. "No. No."

I don't want to miss the split second during which the universe opens up and shows me how to say, *Hi, I'm Leila Abranel and I saw you with my sister and I was wondering, hey, do you know why she did it?*

It doesn't sound so bad in my head, but experience tells me that it's bound to come out horribly wrong. I try to imagine him in a play with his every action transformed into a stage direction. It only succeeds in making me realize that T. may not know anything. His being here is a moment I've imagined as starting a discovery. In the story I have told myself, he's important to my sister and knows her better than any of us. However, it's equally likely that T. was a work associate, that my seeing them together meant nothing, that his being here will only end my hopes.

I am, *Oh, joy,* paralyzed with terror.

And yet, I hover by the table, letting everyone in my section wait just a tad too long for fresh water, checks, and attention. My tips are going to tank today. Eamon actually has to remind me that he asked for coffee.

"You look terrible," he says.

"Nice to hear," I tell him.

In truth, T., despite being as good-looking as I remember, is the one who looks terrible. Sort of drawn around the features, like Da with no sleep. I don't catch much of what he and his friend are saying and what I do hear makes no sense. *Is it helping?* the friend is asking as I put the salad down. Is what helping? And helping what? Who are you? Come on, Leila, come on. When T. hands me his credit card, he becomes a name and, therefore, a person capable of living beyond my questions about Rebecca. He becomes that much more unapproachable.

I bring Adrien Tilden (aka T.) his receipt and carry the dishes away, pausing by one of my neglected customers to answer a question. Adrien Tilden holds open Acca's front door for his friend. I watch, as if from under water, while he turns toward me. His head tilts a little as he considers me, and it takes every bit of everything I've ever had to look right back at him.

It all happens slowly and yet is as confusing as when

things go very fast. In the space of one breath I think he moves in my direction and then everything fades away. There's a heavily moving curtain of black, a sensation of falling, and the sound of someone calling from far away.

I faint.

Only I don't know this, of course, until I stop fainting. Which is pretty much when I open my eyes. Both Hal's and Eamon's faces are hovering way too close to mine. Hal waves his hand in front of my eyes.

"Leila, can you hear me?" he asks.

I nod and he, Eamon, and Drew help me up to a chair. Drew must have caught me because nothing else can explain my head having been in his lap. Did he get the tray? I look around. There's exploded china all over the table I'd been standing near.

"Oh, God," I say. "Did I hurt anybody?"

Hal looks at me with a worried expression and holds up his hand.

"How many fingers do you see?"

Drew, who shares my dread of flying dishes, answers, "No one got hit. I had hold of the tray too, so that everything slid instead of dropping."

I smile at him and say to Hal, "Seven? Eleven? Am I on Mars?"

"I guess you're fine, then," he says. "You scared me."

"I'm—" I don't finish. I'm not going to apologize for fainting. I'm already mortified. Adrien Tilden looks at me and I pass out? Well, I'm a pathetic excuse for an Abranel girl.

"You need to go home," Hal says.

"No, no, I'm fine," I say. Although I'm pretty sure that if I stand up the room will spin around.

"I'll take her," Eamon says. "We'll get a cab."

I see Hal start to speak and then change his mind. He gives me twenty dollars, saying that will cover it and that I'm to call him the minute I get home. The exact minute.

"I'm fine," I say. "Really."

"I've got to go deal with customers," Hal says. "You sit here until you're ready to get up."

I ask Drew for some water and then he and Eamon look down at me with wide, concerned eyes while I drink it.

"Cut it out," I tell them. "I'm fine. Except that now I owe Hal twenty dollars and I am so not calling him."

"It's to make sure I get you there safely," Eamon says. "My being a paying customer doesn't mean he trusts me."

"Good luck abducting her," Drew says. "She's strong for a girl."

He's still fussy because I can lift cases of water that make his back hurt to look at.

"Go away," I tell him, and he gives my shoulder a pat before returning to work.

"We can sit here for as long as you need," Eamon says.

"There's no way I'm taking a cab," I say, looking at my watch.

It's not even six, so the traffic will be ridiculous.

"You are," he says.

"The subway's much faster," I say.

"It's only faster when you haven't fainted," he says.

"What about your father?" I ask. "You can't make him wait."

"While you get your stuff, I'll call him," Eamon says. "Today, he can make other arrangements."

I stand up and the walls stay still. It's all done. I'm myself again. What's important here is that I have T.'s name. A name can lead me to a person. And I'll find a way to stay conscious next time.

Seventeen

I WALK WITH EAMON OVER TO SIXTH AVENUE, where he thinks we can get a taxi. It would have made more sense to head to Eighth, but I'm not up to thinking about directions. Instead, I ask if we can walk a little bit, saying,

"I'll probably get carsick in a cab."

At some point during the next couple of blocks, his hand slips into mine and I'm glad to discover that while the zing-zang-zoom still happens, it's a lot calmer. As if something unusual has become suddenly familiar.

We are waiting for a light when Eamon looks at me and asks if it's okay to ask me something.

"Sure," I say.

"Are you in trouble?"

With whom, exactly, and about what?

"I mean, ah, you know, guy trouble?"

It takes me a half a block to put everything in order

and then understand. I fainted, he's really reluctant to ask me about the reason, and this can only mean:

"I'm not pregnant," I say, thinking how it's been almost six months since that was a danger.

"You're sure?"

"Oh, yeah," I say. "Positive."

I remember Rebecca once telling either Da or William, *I have my period even as we speak,* but decide that Eamon doesn't necessarily want to know that. Weird how you can tell anyone that you're pregnant, but the whole bleeding thing is top secret. The blood simply means your body works. Pregnancy, however, means that not only have you had sex but that you will shortly become a mother. Which is more life altering, and therefore more deserving of secrecy.

"I'm sorry," Eamon says. "I didn't mean to be so nosy. Really."

He looks and sounds as if some terrible mistake has been made. I wonder if I am like Rebecca in that I make people afraid of me. Afraid of intruding on a vast privacy that will turn out to be lethal. I stop walking and literally pull Eamon to a stop. People walking by are in the usual hurry, but we do not appear to be in anyone's way.

"I have a sister," I say. "I did. I mean, I still do have one, but the other one, the one I *had,* she's gone."

I have his attention, and you know, maybe this is the thing I like about him. The way his whole body listens to me. The way anything and everything can and should be said.

"Rebecca killed herself," I say. "No one knows why. It's a mess. Like we all lost the end of a really important story."

"I could be wrong," he says. "But I think no one ever knows why in these cases. That's what makes them so hard."

I consider this. I don't like Rebecca being part of *in these cases.* Rebecca is special and different and unique. But I do like how he doesn't assume he's right. That he knows it's hard. It's hard like math, reading, and directions all rolled into one.

"There was someone at Acca," I say. "Someone who knew her, and I was—I was too afraid to talk to him."

And I almost cry but somehow don't. The idea of Clare and the bathroom and the running water makes a new kind of sense.

"Oh, Leila," Eamon says. "I'm so sorry."

The *sorry* seems to slide into us as he puts his arms around me, and it's nice (the perfect, perfect word for this) to lean against someone and let every bit of misery go into a solid weight that promises to protect you.

One of us pulls slowly away and the other one moves forward and until now I had not given enough thought to how kissing is not always a sex thing. More a words don't work thing and a transfer of affection to make up for how very often *words don't work.*

I'm pretty sure I've never kissed anyone like this right out on the sidewalk and done it because it would be sad not to. Until now, kissing has never made it both harder and easier to breathe.

When we're done, his nose brushes against mine and he says, *Hey, bunny.* And, then, most unexpectedly, "I'm such a jerk." His hands fall away from my shoulders. "I was waiting until June."

And we're back to June again.

"What? Waiting for what?" I ask him, wondering how two people can have the exact same experience but still two entirely different things have happened.

"I don't date teenagers," Eamon says. "I leave that to my father."

His father? Okay, ignore that as being too bizarre. But I've let him believe I'll be twenty soon. That would make me nineteen, which I've always thought of as being beyond a teenager. More to the point, does *I don't date teenagers* mean he wants to date me?

That's what this is about? What happened to flirting not meaning anything? Dating means something, even if people at school almost never do it. I see my sister in all her dark, small glory slipping on high heels, perfume, and powder. She dated William. In secret for a while because she thought, correctly, that Janie would have a fit about William's age and that Da would be silently uncomfortable. Rebecca and William never lived together until they got married. So all that time before counts as dating.

Clare dated Gyula before they turned into a great big love that blew up over a hotel. I remember Clare in my parents' kitchen five years ago. It's my first detailed memory of her. She was looking at Da and saying, with more sarcasm than the world could possibly hold, "Yes, I am. I'm dating what you call a corrupt, ex-communist business tycoon. Dating, dating, dating. Happy?"

I've been certain I wouldn't want to date anyone again until I got less confused about sex. But the idea of turning my body over to Eamon in return for access to his doesn't seem very confusing. Except, of course, for the lie I have told him. If he thinks nineteen is still a teenager, what does he think of sixteen? Or even seventeen, which will be here much sooner than twenty.

"You want to date me?" I ask, trying not to sound the way I do when asking Raphael about math problems.

"Well, I thought I'd take you to dinner and we'd go from there," Eamon says. "You know, if you wanted to, that is."

He laughs, but it's not his real, happy laugh which I've heard while safely inside Caffe Acca.

"Of course, I also thought I'd handle it a little better," he adds.

I handled it badly. One of Clare's chronic comments about herself. As if everything in the world would be different if only she, Clare, had handled it all better. Janie, Rebecca, Da, Gyula, work, and her *inadequate* German. Approaching what she wishes she'd done better, Clare has a fierceness that is alluring as well as alarming.

I can't tell if Eamon is also fierce, but it's something I'd like to know. There's something big and dark behind his silence on topics like his father, his mother, and the last job he had while still in Los Angeles.

We've started walking again, and I am beginning to long for a taxi.

"Handle it how?" I ask.

"With a tad more grace," he says. "And not on a day that you fainted. Or told me about your sister."

"I see," I say, not seeing at all.

"If you like me at all, you'll forget this," he says.

159

"When you come back from Poland, you'll have mercy on me and let me take you to dinner."

And there is the snag. The thing that can't find a place, that throws it all out of order. My birthday will not, as he thinks, stop my being a teenager.

No one ever thought Rebecca was a liar, and opinion was divided on the "rightness" of what she chose to keep secret. But in the end, what she chose not to say, what she kept private, what she let everyone believe—*I'm fine and in no way planning a suicide*—was a lie. Until her death, I'd have been happy to know that anything about me was like my sister, but now . . .

Without my having to ask him, Eamon has stepped into the street to flag down a cab.

"Wait," I say. "Wait."

"I don't think we should walk anymore," he says. "You look pretty worn out."

"Listen," I say. "I do like you. I would have mercy . . . I—Eamon, stop hailing taxis."

He stays off the curb but turns to me.

"I won't be twenty in June," I say. "I'll come back from Poland seventeen."

He looks at me, kind of staring really, and then starts to smile. And then laugh—the real one, but directed at himself. He steps back onto the sidewalk.

"You are," he says. "Of course you are. You are. You're sixteen."

"You thought I wasn't and I don't . . . I almost never lie," I say, unhappy to discover the start of another talking jag when all I want to do is lie down and sleep. "It's not that I'm such a good person, but that I can't keep a lie straight. And it seemed that at twenty I was already too young. And, I, I don't know. Anyway."

"You didn't really lie," he says. "And if you did, I wanted to believe you. Come on, I've got to get you home."

In the cab, I lean against the door. Eamon takes off his jacket, folds it, and leans across to put it between my head and the door. It smells like him and I am reminded of right before the kiss. Of feeling safe beyond measure.

"I guess dinner is out of the question," I say while looking at his profile.

I remember how when we first met, I didn't think he was so good-looking. And he's not when compared to Gyula or Adrien Tilden. Instead, Eamon's features and expressions make you (make me) want to look at him for a long time. He's a little taller than I am, but in the barely way that Raphael is taller.

"Let's just say it's delayed," Eamon says, looking

out the window before turning to me. "I'll turn thirty-one while you're in Poland, Leila. That's still too young for a midlife crisis."

Janie had said that Rebecca was William's delayed midlife crisis. That men were supposed to fall for younger women when they were pushing forty, not when they were facing fifty. I notice how much easier it is to think of Janie than of my sister.

"It is too young," I say to Eamon. "I know. You're right."

"But I do wish," he says, "that you weren't quite so amazing."

I do some quick math, counting on my fingers without looking at them. Eamon's fourteen years older than I am. William was twenty-one years older than Rebecca, a number my sister said she was sick of hearing. Gyula's nine years older than Clare. Which is exactly how much older Da is than my mother.

It's hard for me to believe that any of this is important. William and Rebecca didn't break up because he was older. And fourteen years, after all, is only five more than nine. Of course, my father does not date teenagers, so I'm less likely to be all weird about it. And perhaps Eamon doesn't want to date me with the kind of sharp, pure longing I suddenly feel to slip my hand into his. To ask if he has a middle name or a favorite food. To feel his hand in mine and learn the whole story of his life. It will pass, hopefully it will pass.

"I guess we'll have to be friends," I say.

"We can try," he says, which strikes me as oddly familiar, but I am too tired to guess why.

At the apartment, which he insists on walking me to, Eamon is good with Clare. I listen as he explains what happened at work without making it sound either important or trivial. He writes down his cell phone number on the back of a business card that still has his Los Angeles information on it. And he hands it to Clare, which even I can admire as a bit of brilliance.

No designs on your sixteen-year-old sister, he seems to be saying with every word and gesture. *I'm a guy who was in the right place to do the right thing.* Later, when I think about it, I'll realize that what he seemed to be saying reflected nothing more than the truth.

"Please," he says to Clare. "Call me if I can do anything to help."

Eamon looms over the chair into which Clare has propelled me.

"Be good," he says.

"Okay," I say.

"Call Hal," he says. "He'll worry."

And then he's gone.

"Well, he seems nice enough," Clare says. "Interesting how you like them so low-key."

"It's not like that," I say, wondering if I'm going to throw up as the perfect end to my fainting day.

"I know, I'm teasing," Clare says, smiling and holding her hand out. "Come on, you're going to bed."

And I pitch into sleep without writing down either *Adrien Tilden* or *fourteen years*.

Eighteen

THEY'RE BOTH THE FIRST THINGS I think of, however, when I wake up. Clare took my shoes off but must have decided to leave well enough alone with my clothes. Yesterday seems like something too big for me to think about all at once. The trick to not getting confused by new information is to deal with it one detail at a time.

For example, I'm amazing? I am a lot of things, but *amazing* was a word for Janie. Who was also brave. Which I need to at least pretend to be. After school, which I wish would end already, I march myself into Rebecca's room.

Adrien Tilden's name is waiting for me under *A* in her address book. There are four addresses for him, two different ones here in the city, one in London, and one in Baltimore. They're all crossed out except for the one in Baltimore, which has two phone numbers. One of the crossed-out addresses is a building two doors down from where my tutor lives.

What to do? What to do? His lengthy stay in Rebecca's address book could mean he was important. Even if he can't tell me why she did it, he could probably add to the little I know about her.

I can't call him—what on earth would I say—and don't trust my letter-writing skills. For days I walk around in a fog, trying to judge how important knowing the truth is. Whatever it is, it won't bring her back. But if I could figure out how to contact him, maybe I'd feel better about her being gone. Or not.

And then there's this: Eamon does not show up at Acca on Wednesday or the following Monday. I have his phone number but decide against using it. He's probably decided he has enough friends.

Still, I think about him more than I don't. If I'm not careful, I think about him all the time. What would it take to return to the ease of feeling safe and appreciated? The way I did with him. It would take, I decide, being twenty. Better to think of my dead sister than a man whose kiss I will remember forever. Even if he vanishes as completely as Rebecca has.

Instead of studying for exams, I write *Dear Mr. Tilden*

and *Dear Adrien* over and over until I think to type *Adrien Tilden* into my computer. Fifty-three hits. All of which indicate he's a professor in the Slavic Languages Department at Johns Hopkins. His name shows up a fair amount along with a Russian poet whom Rebecca loved. Adrien Tilden appears to be one of three people whose entire careers are about translating Anna Akhmatova.

Rebecca's poetry books are in the living room where Clare is doing what she always does in the evenings— paperwork. I cast an eye over the shelves until I find the one holding all of the translated Russian poetry. Adrien Tilden's name is on three of the books. I pull them out and find part of what I'm looking for. On one of the title pages, in beautiful handwriting, for all the world to see, is the inscription *For Rebecca, with deepest appreciation, Adrien Tilden.*

Rebecca is here again, doing her routine of *I'm dead, but you can almost see me.*

I look at Clare. Now that winter's over, her flannel sushi pajamas are gone (she's wearing boxer shorts and a frilly tank top), but her glasses and messy blonde ponytail are the same. I know I love Clare, but I knew that before Rebecca died. What's different is that I know Clare better now. My still here sister is interesting and, on occasion, hard to understand. But she is here, after all, and I have as much access to her as I need. As I want.

It's unfair of me, but I persist in wanting to know Rebecca more than I want to know Clare. Perhaps it's because I'm certain that the Clare I know is the one Da, Janie, and Rebecca knew as well. Whereas the Rebecca I knew promised me something that she had refused to the others; without saying it directly, my now dead sister let me understand that one day I would know her secrets.

I sit down next to Clare, who looks at her watch.

"Do I need to be making you go to sleep?" she asks. "Raphael says you're going to do really well."

Other people have always been more interested in my exams than I ever have.

"You'd think he was taking them," I say.

"He's not like Da," Clare says. "He doesn't care how you do, but he says you're the smartest of the Abranel girls and it's just a matter of time."

"Time for what?"

"For it to become obvious," Clare says.

"All that's obvious is how much help I need," I say. "Da should probably send money to Raphael as well as to my tutor."

"The last thing he needs is money," Clare says. "He does it because he loves you."

Well, actually, he does it because he loves you. I leave this as a thought because if I have to tell her that, what is the point? Instead, I hand Clare the book with Adrien Tilden's handwriting in it and ask if she knows him.

"Never heard of him," she says. "But I wasn't the poetry person. Rebecca was really into all this. She even took Russian at some point. I think after college."

"Adrien Tilden knew Rebecca well," I say. "Very well."

"That I doubt," Clare says. "Not even William knew her well."

"You did," I say, but I wonder.

My sisters loved each other, but it wasn't based on their being close so much as it was based on, despite obvious differences, their being the same.

"I knew her within limits," Clare says. "Rather glaring, obvious limits."

And yet, this sameness. It wasn't only because they had the same father *and* mother. It came from years and years of knowing each other just a bit better than anyone else did.

"I saw Adrien Tilden with Rebecca," I say. "And I have this feeling it's important. I can't explain."

"You don't have to explain it," Clare says. "If you need to talk to him, we'll find him."

"There's no point in finding him," I say. "Until I know what to ask. I don't even know what I want him to tell me."

"Well, I've never heard of him and he wasn't at her wedding or the memorial service," Clare says. "So I don't know what he can tell you."

That I don't know either is exactly why it feels so important. I tell Clare about signs and how they make us see what we wish. I say that I wish more than anything that I knew Rebecca better. I amend that with,

"Had known her. For longer or more or closer."

"I think we all wish that impossible wish," Clare says. "But signs are important. We need them. I need them."

"When do you ever need them?" I ask, thinking that when it comes to family facts and secrets she knows most of what I wish I did.

"Well, when you came over on New Year's, you went right to the hotel photographs," Clare says. "I decided that meant you knew what mattered. You were a true Abranel."

I knew they mattered to Da, which is probably why they matter to Clare. For me, they are one more thing that belongs to someone else's story.

"Right then I stopped being nervous," she says. "I knew we would be okay together."

I hadn't thought that Clare was nervous about living with me, but it makes sense. I was as strange to her as she was to me. It's funny what she took as a sign, though. The way I remember that day, she's the one who pointed me in the direction of the lost hotel pictures. I didn't approach the photos on my own, even if Clare remembers it that way.

Exactly why have I decided that Adrien Tilden holds the answers? Because I saw him with my sister? That's not much to go on. Kind of an indirect route to information.

I talked to Eamon because he was sitting at a table near one where Rebecca had been. Look how well that turned out. Now I have another person to miss. Maybe Adrien Tilden is only a sign that it's time for me to know something of my own.

Directly.

Normally I make every effort to steer clear of the whole topic of what has brought me to live with Clare this year. We can easily discuss Rebecca, but not the pills. I will never know a thing if I continue to rely only on what I hear from other people. I count to three. No bravery. Four, five.

"You and Da don't think she had a reason," I say. "Something that made her do it."

My sister takes her barrette out, rearranges her hair, and resnaps the clip.

"I don't think she had a *good* reason," Clare says.

"I don't mean a reason that excuses," I say. "I mean one that explains."

"Look, Leila, I think it's okay if you and I don't agree about . . . about what can be explained."

"So you don't think I'm wrong?" I ask. "Wrong to think that it wasn't just because she was sick."

I don't like the word *depressed*. It's ugly-sounding and if depression kills you then *sick* seems more accurate.

"I think . . . I think it's such a mess," Clare says.

She gets up off the couch, disappears into the kitchen, and comes back with a bottle of water and a plate of cookies.

"I think we each get to decide what happened," Clare says. "My thinking there was no one reason isn't any better than your wishing you knew that one exact thing."

A statement that will need careful examination before I decide if it's true. I ask Clare if she will help me, when I decide the time is right, to write a letter to Adrien Tilden.

"Of course," she says. "But I don't imagine you would need it."

"Da sends my letters back corrected," I say.

Clare makes a laughing-snort type of sound and water comes out of her nose.

"Is he still using green ink?" she asks.

"Yes," I say, glad to hear he did it to them too.

"I thought Mama beat that out of him," Clare says.

"I guess not," I say.

"When you go out into the world," Clare tells me, "no one you meet will have had a father as oddly interesting as ours. That will make up for some of what he does."

"He is what he is," I say, not meaning to quote Rebecca but knowing this is what she would say if she were sitting here on the couch with us.

"God, is that true," Clare says. "Did he ever read to you at night?"

"Fairy tales," I say. "The originals. Where Cinderella's sisters cut—"

"You mean hacked," Clare says. "Hacked their heels off to fit into the slipper."

"All that blood," I say. "I had horrible dreams."

"We did too," she says. "Mama finally hid the book."

Clearly not well enough, although I'm glad that by

simply being himself Da gave me something to share with Julian and Janie's daughters.

"I'll miss you," I say to Clare. "When I'm in Poland."

"You don't have to say that," she says.

"I know," I say. "But I will."

"It'll be empty here without you," she says. "You've made so much of this easier."

Rebecca has faded from the room, taking Adrien Tilden and Eamon with her. From the living room windows, we can see lights glowing across the Hudson. Clare taps her pen against her glasses and I draw my knees up under my chin.

Eventually, one of us will get up.

I have exams, after all, and Clare, as she does every night, has to wash her face, make up her bed, put her papers away, and drink a glass of water. At some point this summer, I will write to Adrien Tilden. She may end up believing that we can't, in fact, each decide what happened to Rebecca. Especially if those versions contradict one another. But until then, we're together. Not the same—never to be the same—but it's enough that we're each still here.

Nineteen

AT ACCA, HAL ASKS ME what I did to scare off Eamon. Only he calls him *that guy who liked you.*

"Nothing," I say. "And he didn't like me."

"Have it your own way," he says. "That guy who you like?"

"It's *whom* you like," I say, sounding for all the world like my father. "And I don't like him."

"So that's why you're looking at the door every time it opens?"

Hal is making fun of me while also letting me know he sees what matters to me. That he's sorry, of course, but would like me to stop looking for Eamon every time someone walks in. In this, Hal and I are united. I too wish I would stop.

And, as soon as my last shift ends, I do. While I'll always love Acca, I'm glad my work here is done. The job was supposed to bring me answers, not more questions.

Clare's insisting on a predeparture birthday celebration.

"I have to go to Vienna and then Sweden the day after you come home," she says. "The trip's going to be a nightmare and I don't want you to be a casualty of that."

Clare got promoted at work. Or rather, as she puts it, Edward has given her the chance to fail by putting her in charge of a hotel in Vienna. She says no one is allowed to be happy for her until it's clear she won't mess it up. I try convincing Raphael to turn the dinner they are planning into one for her instead of me.

"I don't think so," he answers. "This is the birthday that gets lost. It's not sweet sixteen and you can't vote yet either."

Both Da and Janie used to say it was odd how you could vote or join the army at eighteen but not buy a drink. They didn't think that was right.

"Clare wants to make a fuss over this," Raphael says. "And you have to let her."

"I've always liked fusses," I tell him.

"We'll invite Ben," Raphael says.

"Good," I say. "That'd be good."

Now that school is over, the lull between exams and the start of summer plans gives Ben and me a few days to spend time together as we used to. We play cards, listen to music, and look through Ben's collection of industrial design books. We've never read any of them closely, but the diagrams of vacuum cleaners and the insides of the early computers are pretty cool.

Ben's father came across these books on a business trip to Jakarta, where they're printed for an architecture firm. Mr. Greene is a structural engineer and his company does a lot of consulting in Indonesia. During eighth grade, these books seemed like a passport to heaven. Ben and I had this idea that if we could understand those first drafts of good inventions, we'd train our minds to come up with our own brilliant designs.

We've stopped thinking that will happen, but the books are still appealing. Our favorite in the series is an overview of trains with detailed pictures of tracks and steam engines. As we're discussing what could change the world today as much as trains did then, Ben catches hold of the ends of my hair, asking,

"Was it something I did, you know, when we did?"

I look at him wrapping my hair around his fingers. Every serious go-round we had of kissing and everything else would start with his holding my hair. His voice is shaky and I wonder how long he's wanted to ask me about the few days we had of sleeping together.

"It wasn't you," I say. "Of course not."

"It didn't go right," he says. "Did it?"

"That wasn't it," I say. "I mean, I'm better at it by myself, but I . . ."

Something about the way his breath changes makes me pull back and look at him. Everything in Ben's face has just fallen apart. So now I know. You do not tell someone you have slept with that sex is better without them.

Should I have known this? Can I fix what I've done to him? I know how I felt that day on the sidewalk with Eamon. I felt safe and complete. With Ben, I felt far away, curious, and anxious to please.

"It's as if I'm two people," I say. "When we were together, it's like I was different."

"In a bad way?" he asks. "Because I felt different too, but good."

"No, no, not at all," I say, desperate to end this conversation. "Not in a bad way."

"Do you think you'll ever want to again?" Ben asks. "With me, that is."

I can almost hear Rebecca telling me the solution here. She would surely say that I should sleep with him again. That that would be the best way to find out if I can feel with Ben what I did with Eamon. My dead sister, the big believer in acting first and then sorting it out, is perhaps not the person to go to for advice. I try applying Clare's more cautious nature to Ben's question.

"I might want to," I say. "If we thought about it slowly."

"I can think slowly," he says.

When he leans forward to kiss me, I let him. There's no zing-zang-zoom here, but there might be. Maybe. If we think slowly and wait until the summer has ended before we act.

The big-fuss dinner is lovely, with flowers on the table and candles in silver holders. Raphael opens champagne and we drink it from glasses which Clare recognizes as being from her grand-mother's set. Our grandmother, who died before Da's divorce.

"She left them to my mother," Raphael says.

That's interesting, as I'd always heard that Da's mother never forgave Aunt Ingrid for remarrying.

"They were the ones used at Uncle Jacques's wedding," Clare says. "Grand-mere always marked that day.

We'd have dinner at her apartment and drink from these."

"October third," Raphael says.

"The seventh," Clare says.

"Well, it was my mother's first wedding," Raphael says.

"Let's trust your memory, then," Clare says.

"Except I don't remember ever getting together with you guys on that anniversary," Raphael says.

"Believe me," Clare says. "The Barclays were not invited."

"Got it," Raphael says. "Hard to picture my father there."

Ben, who knows I love all the rumors, stories, and details that the Abranels brought with them (along with champagne glasses) from Alexandria, looks at me and smiles. I have drawn him my version of the family chart. Here's my uncle who is dead, here's my uncle who is not my uncle, here are my two sisters, both old enough to be my mother, etc.

As a present, Clare and Raphael give me six chisels, exactly like the ones he has. They are by Robert Sorby and have such beautiful handles they almost look like art instead of tools. Three of them are bevel-edged because everyone needs those, and three are for paring, which will come in handy when we make cabinets for the third-floor guest room.

"Oh, my God," Ben says. "These are perfect."

"It was this or a skirt from Prada," Clare says. "I was overruled."

I've never owned clothes from a "label" before, but these are better. Ben gives me a copy of *Ah, Wilderness,* which the drama club is putting on in the fall. I will, in spite of my hiatus, run the tech crew, so this play is about to become my bible. It's a comedy, which means I won't need to worry about any dark events taking place offstage.

On the card, Ben has written, *Looking forward to building these sets and more of our slow thinking.* I wish that didn't feel like pressure for me to know—quickly—what will happen with us. Even so, I'm very glad he's here. He's like proof that a part of my old life can be in *the new now,* which is no longer new, but simply now.

It's been the first really hot day of the year, and Clare keeps holding her hair off her neck until Raphael brings her a large barrette that looks familiar.

"Oh, bless you," Clare says, her hands winding through her hair as she unsnarls it. "What are you doing with such a thing? Girlfriend leave it behind?"

What's wrong with her? The last girlfriend he had, he broke up with in February. And she was nothing more

181

than an advertisement for how Raphael likes tall blonde women.

"It's your sister's," he says quietly, and when she looks at me I shake my head no, not me.

This, I would like to tell Rebecca, is what happens when you are not here. Because you no longer occupy it, I now share the space you alone used to own.

"She must have left it the last time she was here," Raphael says. "Ben, can you help me with the cake?"

"Sure."

As soon as they leave, I lean across the table and tell Clare that Raphael and his girlfriend broke up. Months ago.

"Really," Clare says, surprise and pleasure crowding into that one word. "Why wouldn't he have told me?"

I think of Ben's note and know immediately why Raphael has never mentioned being single to my sister.

"He knows you know he loves you," I say. "He doesn't want to pressure you."

"No, that's not it, no," Clare says. "No, it's that he used to rely on Rebecca to tell me about him. It's been years since he's told me anything directly."

"He's relying on me now," I say. "And I'm late with the update."

"You think he still loves me like that?" she asks.

"Yes, Clare, I do," I say, so slowly and deliberately that she laughs.

"Rebecca always thought he and I were too clueless to make a go of it," she says.

"You're not clueless," I say. "You're very smart."

"Not about important things," Clare says, looking at Rebecca's enamel barrette before snapping it into her hair. "You know, she'd bought a new space for the store."

"I thought she was just thinking about it," I say. "Making plans to buy."

"Raphael loaned her the money," Clare says. "She closed on the place in October."

October? She got her drugs in August. In October she was seeing people she wanted to say goodbye to.

"How can she have been making two sets of plans?" I ask.

"Two?" Clare asks, getting up to take glass plates from Ben, who whispers, *It's chocolate* to me.

"One to go, one to stay," I say.

Clare sits down next to me, putting her hands on mine.

"I don't know, it'll never make any sense," she says. "But, look, let's keep this night about you. She can't have them all, it's not fair."

But of course she can and it's likely she always will. The trick to Rebecca's shadowing us is to pretend that someday she won't. I can do that and say to Clare,

"I like when your hair is up."

"You and Gyula," she says with a laugh, returning to her side of the table. "But not Raphael or Da. They like it down."

The four of us eat the entire cake (chocolate raspberry, a detail I refuse to see as a sign), which is big enough for eight, maybe ten people. Raphael says that as a scientist, he can confidently tell us that a serving size is strictly in the eyes of the beholder. He somehow cajoles Clare to eat past her two-bites-I'm-done policy.

"It's all in the frosting," he says to me. "It has power over her."

"I think it's a family thing," Ben says. "Leila will eat anything if you add butter and sugar."

"Leila is exceedingly clever," Clare tells him, and Raphael makes us all drink a toast to me and my cleverness.

We use lemon water because no one wants any more champagne and Clare says water toasts are the only kind you can trust. The candles have dripped onto the silver and the napkins look like destroyed party dresses, but I wish I could keep us all here at the table. I'd add

Rebecca, of course, and William because he likes parties. A chair for Gyula, but only if he behaves exactly as Clare wishes. And Janie. Definitely Janie, with my sisters wearing the best of the dresses she bought for them.

It's not until three days later, when I'm on my way to the airport, that I realize I will soon be with the two people I forgot to put on that list.

Twenty

I THROW UP ON THE PLANE. Three times. I tell the incredibly nice flight attendant who keeps bringing me airsick bags and wet towels that I've lost my airsickness medicine. *Airsick* doesn't sound nearly as bad as *consumed with terror.* Especially spoken aloud on a plane these days.

But my terror is the old-fashioned kind, the kind I've always had. The kind that involves crashing or exploding in midair not because of something anyone does but because flying is not *natural*. For years Da has said I would outgrow this theory of mine, but it appears to have, instead, gotten worse.

The apartment in Krakow is nice, with high ceilings and little balconies outside all the windows that face the street. The kitchen is tiny, with a stove that needs a match in order to light, and the huge dining room has the clunkiest-looking table I've ever seen. I guess one person is supposed to cook for a whole lot of people, although I suspect my parents don't use either room very much.

The only food in the kitchen is bread so stale you have to hold it over the stove's flame (no toaster) to make it edible. It's just as well, as I appear to have lost my appetite somewhere over the Atlantic. In my room, my mother has put small plants on the desk, and Da apparently went out and bought me new pillows, saying, *She's very fond of pillows, right?*

He looks better than he did in January. His eyes have regained some of their sharpness, and when he takes off his jacket, he's careful to fold it instead of just tossing it into the closet the way he did the day of Rebecca's service. His ties are all as neatly organized as they were at home, and my mother's briefcase weighs the same thousand pounds it always does.

I spend time looking for and examining their things, as they are not in evidence otherwise. I think they only come here to sleep and shower. There are no books or papers lying around. My mother, who usually leaves her reading glasses everywhere, never once asks me to find them. Normally you can tell where my father has just been because of the half-empty cup of coffee (he only ever likes the first few sips) and uncapped pen sitting nearby.

But not here.

I tag along with them to the hospital for a few days and then buy myself a map and a guidebook and, at a bank, exchange more money. I go out into a city that is not my own and discover two things: I like old buildings, and I have, at long last, figured out my lefts and rights. Clare, who has been teaching me to knit, will be so pleased. Janie taught my sisters to knit, saying that after a thousand stitches, left and right sorted itself out. She knew what she was talking about, and I send her a silent thanks every time I make a turn with confidence.

Most of the buildings I like best are from the 1800s (or were rebuilt then), and some of them are now owned by the church, which I guess means the pope. There are a lot of churches here. A lot as in almost too many, until I remember the pope was born here. He came by it naturally, then.

At first I'm a little afraid to go in any of them (I've never even been to temple), but Da says if you're not praying, it's not like going to church. I'm allowed, he says. He won't get mad. Normally, he thinks that even if older churches and synagogues can teach you a lot about art, the damage religion might do isn't worth what you'd learn. He told my sisters exactly what he's told me: that eventually I'll make my own peace with God, art, and religions. His history being what it is, he himself has no peace. Therefore, he'll leave us to find ours.

Rebecca went into churches all the time, claiming to like the silence. Clare waited outside of them whenever she and Gyula traveled and he went into one.

"I made an exception for the Vatican," she told me. "But I called Da first and got permission. I was twenty-three."

When I wanted to know why she still kept out of churches while Rebecca visited them easily, Clare said,

"Rebecca looked like she belonged to Da's family. I don't, so I guess I'm extra careful before doing anything that makes me less of an Abranel."

I thought I knew what she meant. Because of the way I look, people rarely think I'm Jewish. Or that I'm related to Da, who is the Abranel I know best. The one who was here before my sisters or me. He does not pray, go to synagogue, light candles, or set foot in any of the churches I want to see from the inside.

Which is why I double-check with Da. Not only to ask if I will be allowed into them (that no one will stop me at the door) but also to confirm that he won't mind. With his consent in hand, I break some kind of record by visiting nine churches in one day.

The crucifixes take a little getting used to even though they aren't very different from paintings I've seen. I like the candles and the severely built, dark wooden seats. It's easy to see what draws people here. On the subject of churches, I will probably wind up more like Rebecca than Clare.

My guidebook says there's a Jewish museum in Kazimierz town and I ask Da if he will come with me, but he says those kinds of things are too depressing.

Too dreary.

"They all start with a religious history specific to Jews in that country but end the same way," he says. "With relics from the Holocaust. It's as if being Jewish is only about the belief and the Nazis."

Whenever I've asked him why we're Jewish if we don't believe in God, Da has always said that history trumps religion. And that we have a right to the history even if we aren't observant. I have a few ideas about history, religion, art, and damage. When they're less vague, I'll want to ask him more. But I like that he's so clear about his own ideas.

When I was in sixth or seventh grade, I asked him why people were observant. Half of my class was out of school at Yom Kippur. For a lot of them, it was the first time they were going to observe the fast. This had been widely discussed for days with both dread and excitement. Being observant seemed like a lot of work if you didn't have to do it.

"Religion is for people who need help asking and answering life's questions," Da told me in his most lecturelike voice. "If you need the help, fine, but it's best to figure all that out on your own."

This never sounded like something that was up for discussion, although I wonder if when Rebecca died my father had wished for some of that help. Except I'm pretty sure suicide violates every religious law there is.

"I'll take you to see Auschwitz if you want," Da says, suddenly looking away from his desk. "That at least doesn't pretend to be a history of anything other than death. We can do a day trip."

Um, no. I don't need Raphael to know this is not the year for Da to take me to Auschwitz.

That night Da says he's gotten something for me.

"I ordered it," he says. "It finally arrived at the hospital."

The hospital?

"I had to order it at work," he says. "Connecting to the Internet here is like racing a snail."

"Have you ever done that?" I ask, imagining my father and Jacques as little boys, trying to get snails across a finish line.

I know there are snails in Egypt because a few years ago my mother worked with someone who was studying the effects of snail-related parasites in the Nile.

"Of course," Da says. "That's how I know it's slow to connect."

"No, I meant snails," I say.

"What about them?"

I'm reminded of how very much talking to my father is like taking a test. Hanging over me are the same dangers of misunderstanding or providing the wrong answers.

Da pulls a paper bag from his briefcase and hands it to me.

"It was the first book your sister ever enjoyed," he says.

The Count of Monte Cristo. Great, another book. But then I consider what I'm holding. A book disguised as a present from my father.

Of all the conversations I've overheard, there's one I wish I'd never remember. My mother's favorite book as a little girl was *The Secret Garden.* She'd read it aloud to me many times when I was small, and at some point I decided I wanted my own copy. Mom was thinking of giving me one just like hers—an early edition and therefore very expensive.

"Why bother?" Da asked her. "It's not like she'll read it. She's worse than her sisters ever were."

To which my mother probably said something like *Julian!* I did get a copy, although I was no longer so anxious to have it. He's never given me a book, but he buys them often enough for Clare—endless biographies or short novels translated from French.

"Clare read this?" I ask him. "It was her first favorite book?"

"Rebecca's favorite," Da says, his whole body deflating just a little, before continuing. "It's the abridged version. Skip the first four paragraphs, if you like. They're boring and might be hard to follow. All that happens is a ship docks in France. In 1815."

He's really making an effort, and I tell him I'm so grateful he got this for me and (here's the lie) I'm so looking forward to reading it.

"It's for you to enjoy," he says. "If it brings you one iota of the pleasure you bring me, that will be a lot."

"Thank you," I say.

I put my arms around his neck, being careful to notice the fabric of his jacket, the smell of soap mixed with coffee, and how his beard stubble is all silver even though the hair on his head is still mostly black. I hope it will be many years before memories like this one are all I have left of him.

Twenty-one

I NEVER MAKE IT TO THE JEWISH MUSEUM, which will no doubt find its way onto a list of missed opportunities, but the city has other draws. I go back to wandering around on Kanonicza Street and through the grand square, whose Polish name I have to write down three times before I stop transposing the *y*'s with the *n*'s. Rynek Glowny. Imagine being dyslexic in this language, where the name Casimir is written out as Kazimierz.

Ben phones almost every day while I am here, which is sweet, but also hard, because I don't have a day's worth of things to tell him. There's a limit, after all, to how interesting my favorite buildings are. His parents gave him a calling card, though, and who am I to decide how he should spend it? He tells me funny stories about kids at the camp and I know they must be following him around the way little kids always do—as if he were the Pied Piper.

I hope that by the time I see him again I'll know as clearly as he does what I want for us. In the meantime, I fail to close what feels like a huge distance on the phone.

"It's hard to be on the phone with someone you're dating," Clare says when I mention this on one of my calls home. "Even if you're not totally back together, it's hard."

I decide she knows what she's talking about and not to think so very much. When, on my actual birthday, an enormous arrangement of yellow tulips arrives at the apartment, I assume they're from Ben. Or, as they look very expensive, from Clare and Raphael. My mother carries them up from the ground floor, where the woman who runs the building lives.

We're going out for dinner, so I head to my room to change.

My mother stops me, saying, "Leila, who's Eamon?"

"They're from Eamon?" I ask. "Let me see."

For Leila, who, unlike her name, is as bright as I hope these are. Enjoy the day. In spite of what it's not, seventeen's a good number. Eamon.

The message is a computer printout, but it's still a note. From a man. On my birthday. Gyula's card to

Clare—*So glad you were born. Please allow them*—floats through my mind. I read the slip of paper again.

Although all the words are there, it doesn't say I'm *bright as day*, but it's what I feel like. A shiny blonde-goddess type of flower. How ridiculous I am to be this pleased. There are, I count, twenty tulips. He's gone to some thought and trouble to get them here. I just wish he knew how much I'd rather have seen him again after that day.

"Honey, are you all right?" my mother asks, and I recall her first question.

"I . . . he's someone I . . . he's from work," I say. "From Acca."

"Someone you like?"

"I think so," I say, aware that she's really asking, *Is he important?* "He was nice to me."

"'Was?'"

"He's thirty-one," I say. "He got a little skeevy when he found out I was sixteen."

"I see," she says. "Are you okay?"

"It made me sad," I say, fingering one of the flowers. "But only a little."

"Do you want to tell me about it?" she asks.

I slip the note into my pocket as if to protect it from questioning.

"There's nothing to tell," I say.

"He sent you these because of nothing?"

"I'm fine," I tell her. "Nothing happened. Really."

My mother almost never misjudges what's important. She sees what needs to be done and does it. She's the one who hired my tutor while Da was still screaming at the school for having taken so long to spot the dyslexia. In a way, I'm relying on her judgment. If she believes I'm fine, then I'll know I am.

"I know you to be true to what you want," Mom says. "So I'm not going to worry."

She sounds a little worried. Not about my being fine now, but that I won't be later.

"Eamon in no way wants to date me," I say.

"So it's come up," she says. "Dating."

"Briefly."

No doubt she's remembering our conversation from last August. The one about honoring my body's uncertainty. I should tell her that I've already slept with Ben. In spite of my doubts. And that while I don't intend to spend my life making mistakes, making that one hasn't irrevocably harmed me.

"I want you to promise me that you'll always trust yourself," she says. "Especially when you don't."

There's a gift here bigger than flowers, although I'm

not sure I could put what it is into words.

"I might want to take a year off before college," I say, to test her faith in my trust and because I'm done talking about Eamon. "Or design sets when I get out of college."

"You know, there are apprentice programs," she says. "Maybe not for set design, but things like carpentry are taught to apprentices. It's an option."

"Thank you," I say, but knowing that if I take a year off it will be to find a way to work in the theater.

"Leila, you're not obliged to do what you think we want," she says. "Your father never made that clear to the girls."

As if that were the thing that might have kept Rebecca here. Being true to what she wanted.

"Does Da ever say why he thinks she did it?" I ask. "Like, if there were a specific thing."

Mom finishes arranging the tulips in a vase she's unearthed from the kitchen.

"For him it's bad enough that she did it," she says.

"He seems better," I say.

My mother nods, saying, "He's fighting so hard to keep from being wrecked."

And that is the word for my father. He's not better, he's less wrecked.

"Remember that if she had a reason," Mom says, "it won't help anyone."

"Clare thinks there wasn't any one reason," I say.

"Who knows," my mother says.

I decide against asking if she has a theory. Finding out what other people think isn't going to help. I need to discover what, if anything, other people *know*.

Later that night, after the birthday dinner out, Da knocks on my door.

"May I come in?"

"Of course," I say.

I've been reading the book he gave me. I hope I'll enjoy it but for me reading is work. On this day that I am seventeen, having to work just so as to read feels, more than usual, like a great injustice. My father sits down on the end of my bed, the way he used to when I was little and afraid of the giant spider I thought lived in the radiator.

"Your mother tells me the flowers are not from Ben," Da says.

This is getting ridiculous. Poor Eamon.

"I don't think that the person who sent them was expecting to be discussed quite so much," I say.

"This is the thirty-one-year-old who's feeling *skeevy* about your age."

"Yes," I say.

Yes, yes, now leave it alone. I have a sudden and unwelcome insight into Rebecca's craving for privacy.

"I'm clearly not an expert on women," Da says. "But I know a little about men."

He pauses, looking away for a fraction of a second.

"I think," Da says, "I think that perhaps I forgot to tell your sisters that they deserved kindness from the men they loved."

I consider this. William was kind. And Rebecca left him, telling me she simply could not think with William so anxious to think for her. Raphael is the definition of kind, but Janie thought Clare needed someone a little less anxious to please her.

"Clare benefits from a difficult man," Janie said. "It brings out the best in her."

Maybe Da did forget to tell my sisters to look for kindness, but it seems more likely that other things are involved.

"Don't settle for anything less," my father says. "Never give any part of yourself to someone who is unkind."

Ben is kind. So if I've made a mistake at least it wasn't that one.

"And about college," Da says. "If you want to take a year off, that's fine."

"I haven't decided anything," I say.

"Janie always thought I made too much of this," Da says. "But no one can take an education away from you."

This is a familiar refrain of my father's. My sisters called it *the prison argument for good grades.* Da liked to tell them (and me) that if we ever found ourselves in prison, we'd at least have everything we'd ever read or studied. People can take away a lot, he says, but nothing you *know.*

"I'm not going to go to prison," I say. "I promise."

"When I was your age, I was never going to leave Egypt," Da says. "I knew where my office would be. Which hospital I'd train at. I'd even timed the walk from the hotel."

"I'm trying," I tell him, picking up the book he gave me. "It's hard. If I were meant to have a brain worth taking into prison, wouldn't it be easier?"

I tell him how impossible *Tender Is the Night* was. That I had to read it twice and still needed help in order to figure it out.

"Maybe that wasn't the book for you," he says, echoing Eamon's comments about the book's being a bad fit with me. "But, Leila, the truth is that nothing valuable is easy."

Something to think about, I suppose, on the flight home. My parents' importance could be measured by how much I love them. Or by how very difficult it was to see them.

Twenty-two

ONCE MY JET LAG HAS VANISHED, I call Eamon to thank him for the flowers.

"They made an impression on everyone," I say.

"Your parents, huh?"

"Oh, yeah," I say.

"Sorry about that," Eamon says. "I hope they told you not to make friends with strange men."

No, actually, they said to trust myself and to remember that I deserve kindness. In order for this not to sound too bizarre, I'd have to give Eamon the history of my sisters' love lives, and I don't think any phone call is long enough for that. Instead, I settle for,

"They did not say that."

"Okay," he says. "I won't ask."

"I told them you were horrified by my age and that I didn't think I'd see you again."

"I wasn't horrified, I was being cautious," he says. "Being friends takes more work than dating."

I wonder if I believe that and know I'll have to ask Clare what she thinks before deciding.

"So do I get to see you ever?"

"I'll return to Acca," Eamon says.

I tell him I have a new job. I try to make it sound snazzy, although I know it will be mostly taking messages and xeroxing. I am, I say, interning for a theatrical producer.

"Who is it?" Eamon asks.

Charlotte's never worked in television, which is where he's heard of everyone.

"She's a friend of my sister's mother," I say. "She's doing the new Isaac Rebinsehn play."

Da took Ben and me to one of his plays last year and I didn't like it, but you could tell it was the kind of play that's important. The characters are more ideas than people. In this case, as Da explained, the two halves of Germany when Berlin still had a wall. Plays like that are a nightmare to read, but if you see them it's not so bad.

"Charlotte Strom?" Eamon asks me.

"Yes," I say. "How did you know?"

"My father is Isaac's lawyer."

"So I would have met you anyway," I say.

I think of how Rebecca used to say that the city was really a small town. You could disappear here, but only within limits. Even after switching careers, she was forever running into people she either knew or had heard of from friends. There's no escape, she said.

"It seems possible," Eamon says. "Look, why don't you come to dinner?"

I thought dinner was out of the question. Hadn't he said exactly that in the cab?

"You can meet Dad," Eamon says. "And I'll ask some other people so you aren't bored to tears."

"Really?" I ask, and then, before he can change his mind, quickly add, "Okay."

"I'm glad you're back," he says.

"Me too," I say.

We stay on the phone a bit longer than necessary, not saying anything, until one of us says goodbye.

The night before Clare leaves (and two days before my job starts), I help her pack. She has loaned me some clothes from when she was a size eight (instead of her current six) so that I can go to work looking like I belong there.

"I'll be thinking of you on your first day," she says.

"Do you know what Charlotte does?" I ask.

"No," Clare says, laughing. "Other than light cigarettes she doesn't smoke, I don't."

I pass her a small pile of stockings. We are using my bed, as she still keeps a lot of her things in here.

"You'll figure it out," Clare says, walking over to the dresser.

"Maybe," I say.

She hands me a thin silver bracelet with a pearl clasp.

"I wear this to important meetings for luck," she says. "It's yours for the summer."

It takes me about a week to discover what it is that a producer does. At the end of my fifth day, I make a list of all the people who have phoned the office. Since Charlotte is always either on the phone or in a meeting, I've taken a lot of messages. There is, in the office, both a secretary and an accountant. Even with my answering the phones and doing errands, they are both endlessly busy.

When I am done writing down the messages— union lawyer (*tell her the numbers don't work*), stage manager (*ask her what she thinks about pushing the date back*), Theodore Greyhalle's office (*Isaac's not happy*), landlord of rehearsal space (*returning her call*), the dean of Juilliard (*fundraising question*), casting director (*I think I found the right girl*), director (*I hear Isaac's not happy*)—I have a list of all that goes on before a play can even begin to make its way to the audience.

Until now, I had believed that the invisible part of a performance was the deal between the actors and the audience. But there is a larger, even less visible part. It's the process by which the various technical crews, actors, directors, writers, and all their lawyers come together so as to allow that deal to take place. Each and every night until the play closes, the money is counted and people decide if the results were worth the effort.

"You learn a lot less from a hit," Charlotte says. "But you have a better time."

Until the next play, when everything starts again.

Eamon calls to say that dinner is taking a while to organize and that his father has a meeting with Charlotte's accountant. Would I allow him to buy me lunch on that day.

Yes, I say. I would.

I make every effort not to look forward to it so much, and when I see him, I keep my being thrilled as private as possible. While walking over from Charlotte's office to the park behind the library, I tell him my theory of what is seen and unseen in a play.

"Preproduction is the same in television too. Big and inevitable," Eamon says. "Kind of like an invisible hand. Theatrical instead of economic."

I obviously don't know so much about TV, but it is *not* like theater. However, an invisible hand is a good description. I like that.

"It's economics a little," I say. "The money is important."

"I meant, you know, Adam Smith's invisible hand theory," he says.

"Does he work in television?" I ask.

"No, he had ideas about capitalism," Eamon says. "It's not like I know what I'm talking about. Banking, markets. Not my thing."

We are eating the kind of sandwiches that really need a knife and fork. I wipe off my hands carefully before reaching into a bag borrowed from Clare (leather, silk lining, Italian label, and, I suspect, an old present from Gyula). In my notebook, I write down *Adam Smith* and ask Eamon if capitalism covers both banking and markets.

"Okay, nothing I said was interesting enough to write down," he says.

"I write down stuff I don't know," I explain. "That way I won't forget what I should know."

"What do you do, look it up?"

"Sometimes," I say.

"You're putting a lot of faith in the encyclopedia," Eamon says.

"I usually asked Rebecca when it wasn't a book thing," I say. "She knew."

"Who do you ask now?"

"I just write it down," I say. "That way I can keep an eye on it."

Eamon is looking at me somewhat more intently than he needs to in order to see.

"Okay, so maybe I didn't explain very well," I say.

"No, you explained it fine," he says. "I would suspect that most of the things you don't know come from being seventeen."

"Try from being dyslexic," I say.

"That just means you can't spell," Eamon says. "Or that you read slowly."

"How do you know?"

"I have a nephew who's dyslexic."

"You're an uncle?"

"Many times over," Eamon says.

"I kind of thought you were an only child," I say.

"My father's been married several times," he says. "I have a whole lot of brothers. And they all have kids."

I recognize the way information is being given—the specifics hidden with words like *several, whole lot, all.* Rebecca did this all the time. If you asked what she'd done the previous night, she'd say she spent the day working. This may have been accurate, but it was not the most detailed answer. She usually got around to telling me those details, but only when and how she wanted.

Eamon is claiming some privacy about his family. His father's marriages, his brothers, and their kids are off-limits for now. The trick here is to slide away from the topic without entirely leaving it.

"No sisters, huh?" I ask.

He doesn't answer right away, taking the wax paper and soda cans from our lunch and putting them into the deli bag. His face is hard to read, but he makes me think of Clare on her birthday. Before the breakup, when she was remembering the time Gyula tried to give her a necklace.

"There were stepsisters, I think," Eamon says finally. "I was in boarding school during those marriages and my brothers were in college. I'm not sure any of us knew them."

So the brothers were older. Perhaps not twenty years older like my sisters, but still.

"It was all so long ago," he says.

Decades, I think, remembering Clare's comment about ice-skating when she was little. I put the back of my hand against his, close enough to feel his ring against my fingers. We sit there for a while, hands barely touching. This, I decide, is what I like best about him. The very full quiet. Like on the phone and on the day I fainted. Both before and then right after the kiss.

Eamon uses both arms to look at his watch—the hand of one holding and turning the wrist of the other—while saying, "Okay, bunny, let's get you back to work."

Twenty-three

CLARE COMES HOME FROM SWEDEN and Vienna buzzing with triumph. Work went really well, and I listen to her talk about property location, investors, and exactly how one renovates a hotel in Vienna. I pay very careful attention to what Clare says about work, for there were probably important things I failed to notice when it was Rebecca's career I followed.

A career that is now finally ending, as Clare has found a buyer for the store, something she didn't ever think she could bring herself to do.

"I must be on a winning streak," she says. "I even have an idea for what to do with the money we'll get."

Rebecca left everything to Clare, so it's somewhat inaccurate to say *we* will get anything.

"Provided you approve, that is," she says. "I'm going to check with William and Raphael too."

I know Raphael loaned Rebecca money for the new space in Brooklyn, but why check with William?

"He gave her the money to start," Clare says. "When she left the hospice."

Rebecca had always told me that William disapproved of her changing careers. That he'd said no right-minded person would leave nursing to open a bakery. And yet he gave her the money to do exactly that. I ask Clare which is true.

"Both," she says. "He disapproved and he helped her do it."

"Why didn't you like him?" I ask, a question long overdue.

"She was unhappy with him," Clare says. "That's how it goes. You know, I'll only like Ben for as long as you do."

Since I don't want to think about Ben or how long Clare will like him, I ask about her plans for the money *we'll get*. There's a university in Sweden that is raising money to restore the stained glass in its library's reading room. Clare wants to give them the money they need in return for putting *In memory of Rebecca Jane Abranel, 1963–2001* on a plaque. This is such a bizarre idea that I really like it. But I agree she should check with

Raphael, whom she's already set to meet with so as to keep him in the loop about the sale.

And then the one thing I was certain would never happen does. My sister goes to meet Raphael for drinks and doesn't come home until five in the morning. That's some loop, I think as I sit up in the living room, trying not to fall asleep. I'm not worried, exactly, but it's so unlike her. I think idly about calling the police, but don't.

At one in the morning, the phone finally rings. "Leila, I might run a little late."

"You're already running late," I say. "I've been worried."

I hear her whisper, *She's mad* and Raphael saying, *No, no, let me.*

"As long as you're fine," I say, not sure what to think about all this.

When my sister finally comes home, it's impossible to be mad in any way that she didn't phone sooner.

Clare's already so horrified that they forgot to call and tell me about the sudden change in plans. She's tired. She has to go to work for an early meeting. She's also deeply, endlessly happy. More than the contract for those heated towel racks made her.

"It's the right time," she says. "We've finally found it."

"*You* found it," I say. "It's always been the right time for him."

"No," Clare says. "When I was in law school, he broke up with me."

"I don't believe you," I say. "What happened?"

A question I would never have posed to Rebecca.

"He disappeared, stopped calling," Clare says. "Poof, vanished, you know."

I don't know and hope I never do. Although if Raphael did it to Clare, chances are good someone will do it to me.

"The next time I saw him was at his parents' house," she says. "I was so mad, I wouldn't talk to him."

"For how long?"

"Oh, it went on for ages," she says. "I can really stay mad."

It's not as if he hadn't given her reason.

"Did he ever say why he'd done that?" I ask. "The poof, vanished."

"I think it was the same reason everyone does it," Clare says. "Fear, caution, second thoughts."

None of this seems like a good enough reason to disappear from someone you love.

"So why did you start talking to him again?"

"When I turned thirty, he sent Rebecca and me to Rome," Clare says. "As a present."

Okay, let's see. A trip to Europe from a man you aren't speaking to is allowed. But letting a man who is your great love invest in a hotel your family once owned? That's out of the question. I'll never understand this.

"Of course, Raphael made it seem like we'd be doing him this huge favor if we went," Clare says. "He said if I'd go to Rome, he'd try to fix what he'd done. So when I got back, he and I went out a few times."

When she was thirty, I was ten. Rebecca and William were still married. Did I know about the trip to Rome or the dates with Raphael? Probably not.

"By then, I was already dating Elias, and he was a little more aggressive," she says.

That I can easily imagine. Everyone is more aggressive than Raphael. He was probably still trying to come up with a strategy for the post-Elias Clare when Gyula swooped in.

"When Da called me in Budapest, the first person I wanted to talk to was Rebecca, which was incredibly stupid," Clare says.

It's not stupid so much as it is puzzling. We all

wanted Rebecca—to see, to touch, to talk to—right after she'd made it abundantly clear that she didn't want any of us.

"The other person I wanted was Raphael," Clare says. "I didn't even tell Gyula what had happened until I was home."

I get Clare more coffee, pausing to swirl hot water through the cup just to warm it up. No matter how hot it is outside, my sister likes her coffee scalding. Maybe Gyula was right, I think, when he blamed Rebecca for the breakup. But maybe there's a reason that when she got the worst possible news Clare wanted Raphael instead of her boyfriend.

Raphael calls me that day at Charlotte's office.

"Leila, I feel terrible we worried you," he says.

I pause, wondering if I should tell him congratulations. As happy as Clare is, he must be ten times more so.

"You have to let me buy my way out of this," he says. "I get you something hideously expensive and you forgive me."

"No, it's fine," I say. "Don't even think about it."

"I've made up my mind," he says. "Buying forgiveness is what my father would do."

"Since when do you want to be like Uncle Harold?"

A question that just slips out. Even when I'm really angry with Da, I don't want to hear anyone else criticizing him.

"It's Rebecca," Raphael says, interrupting my useless regret. "When I thought of this ever happening, I knew I would buy her the huge, happy thing I could never give Clare."

It's always Rebecca, I think. I really need to be writing Adrien Tilden.

"You can get Clare something," I say. "You're not Gyula. It's not the same."

"Money is tricky," Raphael says. "You'd be surprised."

Here are some things I know about Clare and money that I didn't know before moving in with her. She almost didn't leave the law firm to work for Edward because of the pay cut. Clare was terrified of winding up as broke as her mother had been before her lighting career took off. I've also found out why Clare and Gyula fought about money.

"The money I earn is to keep me safe," my sister said. "The money he earns gives him power over others."

I would guess that Raphael's money, largely inherited, makes my cousin nervous. He clearly spends it to keep himself and others safe, but I'm sure he's chronically aware that he has more than most people. I don't think Clare would ever suspect Raphael of trying to buy her, but she'd probably prefer he didn't try.

"I guess I could use a present," I tell him, hoping that when I earn money it'll keep me safe without making me nervous, suspicious, or afraid.

All this happens days before the July Fourth weekend. Raphael wants us to spend it at his house in the mountains. He bought it when his father died and has been plotting for years to take my sister there. But Clare thinks we should stay in the city. She says as long as there are alerts for another possible hit, she wants to be here.

"This is my town," she says. "No one's running me out of it."

As if by staying she has some kind of say-so in what will or will not happen. She still gets upset every time she sees flags hanging where they didn't used to be. I like seeing them even though they remind you of nothing but change. I personally don't have anything against running away, but Clare's wish rules.

Everyone but us appears to be leaving for the holiday. Charlotte is going to the Hamptons and so is Eamon.

"Dad loves it there," Eamon says. "He almost had to give it to my mother in the divorce, but she decided it would kill him to lose it."

I've gathered that if the situation had been reversed, Mr. Greyhalle wouldn't have been as generous.

"You'd like it," Eamon says about his father's house. "There's a terrace and a view of the ocean, like your hotel."

"It's Clare's hotel," I say.

Da and Aunt Ingrid's really, but the idea of it belongs to Clare.

"It's a perfect place to work," Eamon says, which I know is important.

The cable network that hired him to turn the Japanese show into an American one has approved his premise and character sketches and now wants a pilot script. The show sounds odd, but not as odd as Eamon's last show, which was about aliens, monsters, and a crusade against evil.

"I might call from there, is that okay?"

"Of course," I say. "Why?"

"Why? I don't know, maybe I'll miss you."

I hadn't meant why would he call, but why wouldn't it be okay. I'd love if he called. Eamon's phoned at the office three times and taken me to lunch twice. I like when he calls. I know there's no dinner date or *going from there* waiting for us the way there was when I worked at Acca. But being with Eamon still makes me feel as if something is about to happen.

Maybe this is what Christmas and Chanukah feel like.

So, of course I want him to call, but I also know he can't miss me. *I miss you* is how Ben ends all his e-mails. Including the last one giving me a list of all the computer gadgets I might ask Raphael to buy. Since I don't want a scanner or a CD burner, I ask Eamon.

I tell him that my cousin—well, my sister's boyfriend who is my cousin except he's not and someday I'll draw the chart—but the point is he wants to give me something. A big and happy thing that I don't need. Any thoughts?

"I take it he'd like to give your sister something but can't yet," Eamon says.

"I think so," I say. "Yes."

"Time is a nice thing," he says. "Clothes get old and computers break. You could ask for his time."

I could ask for more of yours, I think, but no. That would just make everything weird and odd. Even if I can't always figure things out, I'm aware that for him being friends is taking more thought and care than dating would. He's mostly the same, but I don't think it's easy. My job is to keep buried whatever part of me likes him as more than a friend.

"Have a fun trip," I say, after approving his gift suggestion. "Enjoy the ocean."

Twenty-four

RAPHAEL'S TIME TURNS OUT to be exactly what I want *and* need. Now, how often does that happen? Since returning from Poland, I have been on an anti-dyslexic schedule. Each night, after thirty minutes of knitting and math review, I read ten pages of *Monte Cristo*. I will be done with the book in forty-three days. I rarely need the dictionary but I'm not enjoying anything yet.

My father and my tutor claim that people read for the company. That a book is like a friend. The characters seem real, they say, and their story important.

Not so much for me.

If reading is a struggle, it's lonely. It's just you, the dark cloud of *Huh?,* and the few glimmers of *Oh, yes. I see.* I tell Raphael that his present should be to read with me. That way I'll have company even if this guy in *Monte Cristo* stays in prison forever.

Clare picks up the book, scanning the cover.

"Da told you this was her first favorite book?"

I nod.

"It was, but he'd given her the unabridged version," Clare says. "Mama had to put up a huge fight to get him to give her this one."

My sister should be the one to meet with Adrien Tilden and try to shake Rebecca's secrets free. Clare was the one who knew her, all the details belong to her. My Rebecca is like Clare's hotel, an idea more than a reality.

And yet Da was the one who knew that hotel inside out. Only he's a doctor now and it's Clare whose entire work life is defined by her idea of that hotel. That's worth considering. Because who is to say that my idea of Rebecca is less powerful than Clare's vivid and factual reality?

During most of July, I see that I had been wrong when I thought Gyula suited Clare. They had certainly gleamed and glittered, but they didn't quite fit the way my sister and Raphael do. They're almost the exact same height and, when not working, can each be found either reading or staring intently through their glasses at nothing.

Janie was right when she said that Raphael was anxious to please Clare. But this judgment, while clever, missed two things. One, Raphael is anxious to please everyone. It's who he is in the same way that Clare is someone who is blonde. Two, Clare accepts Raphael's efforts to make her life nice. Unlike with Gyula or at work, my sister doesn't need to prove how well she can do on her own.

At first, I worried that things would be different now that Clare and Raphael were together instead of just unrelated cousins. Instead, everything is easier. Except for Thursdays, Raphael stays at the apartment on weekdays. They sleep in the living room and I make a point of not going in there after saying good night. On the weekends we either go to the house in Brooklyn or the mountains. The drive there takes forever, but Raphael lets me fix the back porch stairs and finish some pantry shelves. We're going to build Clare a window seat and walk-in closet for their bedroom.

I have a plan to make the side porch, which is screened in, bigger than it currently is. I unroll my sketches and measurements and show Raphael with a *voilá*. He is suitably impressed and asks if I would be interested in helping him put in a half bath right by the kitchen. He'd have to teach me some plumbing, but we'd have fun.

"Yes," I say, and then add, "Yes, yes!"

At dinner, Clare listens to us talk about framing, wiring, and floor installation.

"I think Leila loves this house more than I love you," she says to Raphael while passing me the bread.

His face gives away that it's the first time she's said it. He must have thought, during those years when she wouldn't talk to him, that he would never find a way back to her. It makes the whole falling in love thing a little less scary to see that mistakes can be reversed.

"What is it about Thursdays?" Eamon asks me. "Where's Raphael then?"

I've been keeping him partially updated about the changes going on at my house. We've taken to meeting on Wednesdays at Acca. His father still has physical therapy and I get off work in time to go downtown and meet Eamon. I am, he likes to say, the highlight of his week.

I think that's only because outside of work his

days are pretty much devoted to making a sick man feel healthy. Not so thrilling. And even though I am his highlight, he always tells me—every Wednesday—that I should find someone better to hang out with.

"Raphael's at home Thursday nights," I say. "Clare needs time to herself."

"Is he that annoying?"

"No," I say. "Of course not. But you know, her last boyfriend was hardly ever around. She's more used to being alone."

Clare calls Thursday nights having a date with herself. We usually wind up with my making dinner and then eating it while seated on the floor. She likes to play gin rummy and drink enough water to drown a fish. I'm learning to hoard low cards and have beaten her a few times. She says I'm a better player than Rebecca. Maybe so, but probably not as good a cook.

"What happened to your hand?" Eamon asks, putting his coffee cup down and pointing toward my right thumb.

I stop eating chocolate raspberry cake and look at my rather impressive bruise. It's of the blackish-blue and orange variety.

"Hammer," I say. "Bang, oops, missed, hit the wrong nail."

I screamed so loudly I almost gave Raphael a heart attack. I definitely woke Clare up from her nap.

"Let me see," Eamon says, taking hold of my fingers.

It is the first time this summer that he's touched me on purpose. It's still there, though, the zing-zang-zoom. Being desperate to hide it makes it a little worse than before.

"It's nothing," I say. "Building stuff, you know."

I pull my hand away, he signals Drew for the check. Everything goes safely back into place.

I had always thought that being in love made people create a world of their own with space for only two, but my sister and Raphael bring everyone into their new, sharp attention. It's as if finding each other at long last has made them even more capable than usual. There's nothing they touch that doesn't seem easier as a result.

The letter to Adrien Tilden? Done. Raphael listens to my description, looks at the address book, the book of translated Akhmatova poetry, and considers the fact that Clare has never heard of him.

"We want to treat him as if he were an old friend,"

Raphael says. "Without assuming anything. Polite, warm, no pressure."

"What if he's an old boyfriend?" Clare asks. "Or worse, what if he doesn't even know she's dead?"

"What if he could tell Leila why he was with Rebecca that day?" Raphael asks. "It's clearly important to her."

"I just don't want you to be disappointed," Clare says to me.

"Little late for that," Raphael says, meaning, I think, that when Rebecca killed herself we were all, among other things, disappointed.

The three of us sit down with paper and come up with the following:

Dear Adrien Tilden, Allow me to introduce myself as Rebecca Abranel's sister Leila. I have reason to believe you were a friend of hers and at the risk of being intrusive I wonder if I might, at a time that is convenient for you, ask you about her. As I am significantly younger than Rebecca, my knowledge of her is limited and I would gratefully welcome the opportunity to increase it. Thank you in advance, Leila Abranel.

It doesn't sound like me, but it does sound like us, and it will never get in the mail if I wait until I write it entirely myself.

With that done, they even find a way (without trying) to help me clear up how I feel about Eamon. His invitation for dinner to meet his father and *some other people* finally materializes and while Clare says something like *Oh, fun, let's buy you a dress,* Raphael has other ideas.

"This is that guy who called here about sending flowers to Poland?" he asks.

"Yes," Clare says. "I've met him. He's very nice."

"I haven't met him," Raphael says.

"Oh, my God," Clare says, laughing. "If you were her father that might actually matter."

"Clare, are you really going to let Leila go to some man's house?"

"She has *coffee* with him," my sister says.

"Cake," I say. "He has coffee."

"It's a place where everyone knows her," Clare says. "It's not like they're up to anything."

"I'm sure she's not," Raphael says.

"It's not 'some man's house,'" I say, not loving the implication here. "It's his father's. His father knows Charlotte and she knew Janie so it's practically like we know him."

"Practically isn't good enough," Raphael says.

"It is for me," Clare says.

"Well it probably isn't for Eamon," I say. "I think

he's been dying for someone to tell me how wrong it is for us to be friends. If you tell me, maybe he'll shut up about it."

This seems to soothe Raphael a little bit, but he still insists that Eamon come over one night.

"He's taking care of his sick father," I say. "How is he supposed to do that and be here?"

"He'll figure it out."

"You're acting like there's only one reason he'd want to be around her," Clare says.

"I'm acting like I don't trust men," Raphael says, which makes her laugh so hard, I know I'm going to have to tell Eamon my guardians are demanding a meeting.

"About time," he says. "I was beginning to think your parents had left you with the most irresponsible people on earth."

What I would like to know is why, if we're just friends, it's irresponsible for Clare *not* to think the worst. And then, perhaps later than another girl would, I see why this is hard for him. If I were that mythical twenty, he'd ask me out. Which probably means he likes me more than he wants to. Not exactly as I like him, but also in a hidden way.

And so, before he arrives to get looked over, I take my secret out and examine it. I like him the way I have never liked Ben, which makes me sad for Ben, but it's too glaringly true to ignore. I like Eamon the way I might have liked Gyula, if he'd ever wanted to be friends with me. A combination of curiosity, alarm, and flat-out glee.

Okay, then. I can live with this. Even without knowing anything about what Eamon's hidden away. I doubt that the way he likes me involves any alarm or glee, more a kind of reluctance, but it's enough that he might or would like me at all. If I were totally different—smarter, older, whatever.

Twenty-five

THE VISIT FOR EAMON TO MEET my wannabe parents takes place on a Sunday afternoon. A family friend agrees to spend an hour or so with Mr. Greyhalle, who doesn't need chronic observation so much as company. We come back from the mountains early and Clare goes out to buy chocolates and pumpkin bread. Raphael promises me no one will be *awful*.

"You're very good to let me worry about you," he says.

"Yes," I say, thinking that if he can keep on making Clare happy I'll let him do anything.

Eamon's talent for putting people at ease, which I first observed at Acca, also appears here. It turns out that the last TV show he worked on was one of

Raphael's favorites. The show about aliens, monsters, and fighting evil was, they tell me, a huge hit with what Raphael calls *inept science types*.

"Well, no wonder I never heard of it," Clare says. "I'm not a genius science type."

I love Clare for transforming Raphael's *inept* into *genius*.

"She didn't have cable until two years ago," Raphael says to Eamon.

Because Rebecca insisted. I remember that discussion when my sisters moved in together.

"Leila's not a big fan either," Eamon says. "Do you even like movies, bunny?"

"Everyone likes them," I say, trying to think of the last one I saw. "Of course."

"She's like my mother," Clare says. "Loyal to the stage."

"It's a dying art," Eamon says. "Even my father will tell you that."

"What did Janie always say?" Raphael asks Clare. "Only a dying art can demand your whole life?"

Eamon tells us that while this may be an admirable point of view, he has nonetheless invited some people to his father's for me to meet. A production designer because I like to build sets and a producer, who is a lot like Charlotte, although she works in TV. Movies also. I may find, he says, that only working in theater is limiting.

"Leila seems very ambitious," he says to Clare and Raphael.

I'm not, but they both agree with him so quickly that I wonder. Well, there are things I want, goals I have, and I do work to get them. I thought only people like Clare or my mother, with easy-to-spot careers, were ambitious, but I see how it might fit for me too.

Clare says that from the moment I saw my first play, I announced that I was moving into the theater. I have no memory of this, but it feels right. Eamon is telling them that when we first met, I was reading a book for school and,

"I've never seen anyone quite so intent on conquering something," he says. "Very impressive."

"She's always been really determined," Raphael says.

I wish they would stop discussing me like this. Enough already.

"You know, when I was seventeen, I was wandering around India," Eamon says. "Looking for my life."

Apparently a common thing to do in India, for they have a little discussion about temples, chanting, and the benefits of travel over meditation.

"I went to Thailand and Cambodia after college," Raphael says. "I almost stayed. What finally brought you home?"

"I met one too many people who thought searching was living," Eamon says. "I promised myself I would finish school and always have a job."

"I came back for grad school," Raphael says. "Work's very handy when you're looking for meaning."

"That's true even in television," Eamon says.

"Rebecca used to go to an ashram in Massachusetts," Clare says. "She thought of maybe going to India one day."

Something in her voice catches and Eamon quickly steers the conversation away from Rebecca and her useless plans for the future.

"So my thoughts were that if I can help Leila meet people who can really help her . . ." he says. "Well, you know, that would, that would be good."

He may be making Clare comfortable enough to have an unguarded Rebecca moment, but he's not having nearly the easy time he had when he was last here. Raphael asks how Eamon's father is doing. Which is how I find out that Mr. Greyhalle is seventy-one. How can he be only four years older than

Da? Mr. Greyhalle's already had cancer, broken his hip, contracted viral pneumonia, and almost started a fire by forgetting to turn the stove off. When Eamon says, *Dad's just got old age catching up with him* I think my heart is going to stop.

"It's a lifetime of bad habits," Eamon says.

Well, Da has good habits. Does he? Doesn't he? If anything happens to Da, my life will crack into a much bigger *new now* than it did when Rebecca died. I remind myself that my mother is with him. I calm down. Eamon is saying,

"My father's not ready to hire help, so I'm the next best thing."

"That's got to be stressful," Raphael says. "Does he resent your helping him?"

"The stress is nothing compared to turning a Japanese cartoon into an American episodic," Eamon says.

I recognize a nonanswer when I hear it and I know how much Rebecca would have liked him. I also understand—as clearly as I know anything—that if she were still alive, Eamon and I would never have met. Why is it that the things I know give me a bigger headache than the things I don't.

The visit ends with Eamon's drawing a floor plan of

the monster-haunted castle from his old TV show and Raphael making a beautiful drawing of the DNA in the disease his lab is analyzing.

"Well, it was very nice to meet you," Eamon says, standing up. "And not nearly as awkward as when I met my prom date's parents."

"Yeah, sorry about that," Raphael says.

"No, not at all," Eamon says. "You should know her friends."

And just as he is smiling at me, Clare, obviously possessed by one of the aliens from his show, says,

"We weren't vetting you or anything. I mean, we trust Leila to make her own decisions about dating."

"Okay, now I feel awkward," Eamon says. "Is this where I need to tell you I have a girlfriend?"

"You do?" This comes out all shocked-sounding, and I decide I must also be possessed.

"Not helping," Eamon says to me.

"No, look, I'm sorry," Clare says. "Really, all I meant is that, in this state at least, you know, the age of consent is seventeen."

"Also not helpful," Raphael says.

Clare looks from Raphael to Eamon and then back to Raphael, who starts to laugh. Clare looks horrified with herself for being so weird. Age of consent? Hello, there has to be sex involved before that becomes important. And before that he'd have to ask me out.

For that matter, I was still months away from seventeen when Ben and I slept together. Did he break the age of consent, or does being the same age give you an escape clause? Funny that there should be laws about all this.

"I'm sure that's useful to know," Eamon says. "But what with my father and work, I'm kind of overly occupied for dating."

And yet he was not too occupied in April. And May. Does this mean he's lying now or didn't mean it then when he said he wanted to take me out to dinner? Or did dinner and going from there not mean *dating*? Dinner, presumably, would be legal at any age.

It doesn't matter. He's called me ambitious and impressive. He's sat here for an hour. He wants to introduce me to people whose work I might learn from. I've had great friends, but Eamon is outdoing himself.

"I'm so sorry," Clare says again. "That came out all wrong. Rest assured, Leila will kill me as soon as you leave."

"Are you kidding?" Eamon asks. "She thinks you

walk on the moon. Nothing you say to me is going to change that."

Clare looks at once embarrassed and pleased. I'll always be in Eamon's debt for being the one to tell Clare that she's important to me.

Before my parents left, I remember being slightly alarmed by how indirectly news flowed to and from Clare, Da, Raphael, and even William. But now, this business of giving and receiving information through third parties makes sense. Or feels familiar. It is, I'm certain, part of why I know anything about Eamon. Why I've been able to be friends with him. It's all taken place softly, the way being with Rebecca did.

I could see almost right away that Eamon kind of clams up under direct questioning. However, thanks to my sisters, I'm very good at getting information from people who guard it. Since my return from Poland, I've learned where Eamon went to college, the names of his eleventh grade English teacher, his first girlfriend, and his brothers, ages forty-seven, forty-five, and forty.

Eamon's mother was Mr. Greyhalle's second wife (there were two after her) and she now lives in Boston, where she teaches third grade. Her parents, dead for almost twenty years, lived in Ireland, and Eamon is named after his grandfather.

"She was supposed to be Dad's trophy wife," Eamon said about his mother. "But she had the wrong personality."

It's amazing what people will tell you when you are in the midst of discussing their work. Work does not make him quiet. He has a lot to say about television—its function as entertainment, why he can't write for sit-coms, what you lose with a mass audience and what you gain. Buried and revealed in all this are tiny details about him, which are important to me. Because, like Clare, he is important.

Interesting how all the people I love have work at the center of their lives. Work which is the biggest piece of who they are. My mother, Janie, Clare, and especially Da, if you look at his *save the world* jobs. Not Rebecca, though.

Although she worked long, hard hours both at the hospice and the bakery, I never felt that she was passionately attached to either. Perhaps my sister was just unlucky and never found her version of Mom's lab or Janie's lights. Maybe she should have kept looking, a thought that clearly failed to occur to her.

Twenty-six

AT THE START OF AUGUST, Charlotte decides to stay with the revival that's losing money but pull out of the Isaac Rebinsehn play. She feels terrible, since this is the first time she won't play a critical role in bringing his work to Broadway. However, Isaac has already caused one director to quit and the actors he wants are, in Charlotte's view, *all wrong*.

"Ever since that monster-hit in London, Isaac's abandoned the concept of a group effort," Charlotte says. "The Brits ruined him."

Although her accountant calls it misguided loyalty, Charlotte insists on lining up money people (called *angels*) to replace the amount she's pulling out. As for the rest of her job—doing everything that matters other than investing the money—she says her partners can find someone else to do all of the work for all of the blame.

"I feel old," she tells me. "It used to be I stayed ahead of change much better than this."

Eamon's father, who still goes to his office for two or three hours in the mornings, calls her, trying to broker a peace.

"Listen, Theodore," I hear her say. "You're too late for that."

There are other projects in the pipeline, and the phone never shuts up. Underneath the din, though, one can sense Charlotte's quiet gloom. It's clear that one huge drawback of having work that matters to you is that it can break your heart as easily as a great love gone wrong.

On the day of Eamon's dinner party, I get a letter in a blue airmail envelope. It's not from my mother, who writes every week, but an address in London.

Dear Leila (if I may), Thank you for your note, which was just now forwarded to me at my flat here. I will be back at Hopkins by mid-October and would be more than happy to meet with you at any time thereafter. You are certainly welcome at my home or office, but if necessary I could come to the city. Rebecca's death came as a shock and I cannot even begin to fathom your loss. Please know that my thoughts are with you and Clare during this time. I look forward to meeting you upon my return. Cordially, Adrien.

At the bottom of the page, he has written his e-mail address, his two numbers in Baltimore, and a number in London, with the words *rarely in* next to it.

I was right, I think. He knows Rebecca's death has been a loss. Adrien Tilden is a sign I saw because I wanted to, but that doesn't mean he isn't also a real one. And yet I have to face the fact that if he knew anything, he'd have written it. Or phoned. But maybe it's a small thing he isn't sure caused it, but that I'll recognize as being . . . what?

I'm really grasping here and read the note again. He knows Clare's name. Is that proof that he knew Rebecca even better than I'd hoped? I reach for the phone and dial Clare's office.

"Honey, knowing who I am doesn't mean much," she says after I've read her the note.

"Are you sure?" I ask. Only those who know me well have heard my sisters' names.

"There are people I've worked with in Germany and all over Budapest who know I had a sister named Rebecca," Clare says. "I don't think any of them know me. Not in an important way."

"I just can't believe Rebecca didn't talk to someone," I say. "It's not natural to make that big of a plan all alone."

"I know," Clare says. "I wish she hadn't."

This, as usual, is pointless.

"I have to go," I say. "And pour myself into that dress of yours."

Said dress is dark blue with thin shoulder straps and tiny pearl buttons along the sides. It is, my sister has assured me, *casual but elegant.* Even after taking it to the tailor for letting out, it looks like it has been sewn onto my body. There's just so much of me.

My legs and arms are all endlessly long, and if I could I'd tape my breasts down. I'm not *super skinny* the way anyone this tall should be, so I have to settle for *good enough.* There's room for improvement in every female body, and as my mother never tires of saying, if I didn't need a bra I'd be unhappy about that.

I am, at least, having a good hair day.

Eamon said to come at around seven, but of course the number nine sits on the track at Forty-second Street for almost twenty minutes, waiting for trains ahead to clear. On top of that, when I get out at Twenty-third, I cross the street instead of heading south. Not dyslexia this time, but habit. Ben lives in the direction I'm going.

I have to do something about Ben. If Da thinks I deserve kindness from someone I love, then it stands to reason that anyone who loves me deserves the same. I haven't been unkind to Ben, at least not yet. Although if he liked someone the way I like Eamon, the word *kind* might not rush to mind. Even if the girl he liked didn't like him back.

I turn around and head west toward Mr. Greyhalle's apartment. The mirror in the lobby tells me that the detour I took in sticky August-in-the-city air has not done wonders for my appearance. My good hair is gone and now my dress looks soggy.

Deep breath.

I'm the last to arrive, but no one seems to mind. Mr. Greyhalle is as nice as possible, as Eamon said he would be. He pretty much does everything Eamon told me he would, including saying that I'm far too lovely to waste any time with his son, who has no taste.

"Thank you, Dad," Eamon says. "Leila, what would you like to drink?"

"Freezing cold water," I say, which makes a woman sitting over by the window laugh.

She has short dark hair and is wearing big, dramatic jewelry. She's striking more than pretty.

"He's actually a wonderful boy," Mr. Greyhalle says when Eamon hands me a glass full of ice water. "I'd be lost without him."

That's unexpected, since Eamon usually makes his father sound like someone he can never please.

I get introduced to everyone and only remember two names. The striking woman is named Brett Collodi. And then there's Isaac Rebinsehn himself, which is oddly thrilling. Even if he's broken Charlotte's heart and written plays I don't love, he has won two Tonys. More than that, he has made a whole life out of providing the play itself. Without it none of the other work can happen. I shake his hand and say how much I enjoyed his last play.

"And what did you enjoy about such a dreary night?"

I remember now—too late—that as Da was explaining what the play was about, he mentioned that it was one of Rebinsehn's few critical failures. We'd gotten tickets at the last minute because it was about to close.

"Well, I thought you really captured the friction between privilege and oppression," I say, dredging up one of my father's comments.

It works. For a second I think Isaac Rebinsehn is going to kiss me, but he just puts his hands on either side of my face, saying, "Delightful! Where did they find you?"

"Be careful, Isaac," Mr. Greyhalle says. "She works for Charlotte."

Isaac drops his hands and steps back like I'm made of toxic waste.

"Leila, come sit here," Brett Collodi says, moving over on the couch. "Let the old men go off and talk business."

"Ouch," Mr. Greyhalle says to her, and to Eamon, "I told you not to invite her."

"You know you love me," Brett says, smiling at him.

As I pass Eamon I hold my empty glass up and mouth the words *More, please.*

"I've been ordered to tell you how I love working in film," Brett says to me. "But I'd much rather find out what you're interested in. Then I'll brainwash you."

She has the warmest laugh and an intense gaze that mixes a welcoming air with sharp calculation. She is, I decide, Clare without formality. I tell her that plays have always unfolded easily for me and given up their secrets and, odd as it sounds, invited me to help make them real.

"I never read a play without seeing how it would be in a theater," I say. "I do like movies, of course, but all the work is done for you."

"How about when you see a play?" Brett asks, smiling thanks to Eamon, who has refilled her wineglass and brought me an entire pitcher of water.

"I told you movies," Eamon says. "She's already well informed about theater."

"Go away," Brett says. "You have people to feed."

"Is it too late to ask you not to be quite so bossy?" he asks.

She laughs, saying, "It was too late years ago."

"Brett," he says. "Be good."

"Aren't I always?"

And while they are having this lovely, private moment, I consider the water pitcher with its ice and slices of lemon. I want more than anything to dump it over my head. Or hers. His. Perhaps theirs? I'm not feeling too picky.

I look over at two men and another woman who were described as friends of Eamon's from his last TV show. I don't have to sit here. I could go and ask them all about aliens. As Eamon returns to the kitchen, Brett puts her hand on my wrist.

"We haven't been together for years," she says. "But he can still make me do anything. So be warned. That's what will happen."

I just look at her. If I need a warning, I probably won't take it from someone I hardly know.

"I think the whole TV and film thing is his ploy to get you to California," Brett says. "I figure you have to go to college somewhere, and with Charlotte Strom on your résumé you could easily get work that helps you decide if film interests you."

She goes on in this vein for a while as we all move into the dining room, where Mr. Greyhalle holds out both my chair and Brett's. She is forgiven, I guess, for calling him old. Once everyone starts eating, separate conversations break out around the table. Brett is telling me how it's true that in a film all the work is done for the audience.

"But that's the magic," she says. "That's why people will always love film."

I can't tell if I like or hate the way she uses the word *film* as if every movie ever made was a work of art.

"If you become part of the work which a film demands," Brett says, "then you are the magic."

From underneath her avalanche of information, I pull out what seems most relevant to me.

"Why would he want to get me to California?" I ask, my voice suitably low since Eamon is seated across the table from us.

Brett, who had been leaning in a little too close,

pulls back a little before leaning in again to say, "God, he's a secretive bastard, isn't he?"

"Not really," I say. "He's been pretty clear with me."

"I wonder," she says.

"Well, I don't," I say, wishing I hadn't thought so many nice things about her at the start of the evening.

Under the guise of really being curious about *film,* I manage to get her talking about her most recent job. It was, she says, a brutal shoot in Texas. God help her, Texas. The film's being edited now and maybe that will save it. It's the last time she works with that director. Couldn't keep to a schedule or a budget.

When she is quite done, I listen in on some of the other conversations. Isaac Rebinsehn is saying unpleasant things about Charlotte in response to a question about how the new play is going. I wonder if I should point out that my boss has left him in very good financial shape, which is probably more than he deserves.

"He's gotten so out of control," Brett says to me in a whisper. "But look, even Theodore knows what really happened, so don't stress yourself out."

So I think I like her, but I'm in no hurry to decide.

The talk soon turns to a singer whom even I've seen on television. She's been around for a few years, is hyper-cute, and has one of those *ooohh ooohh* love songs playing on the radio. The woman next to Eamon, whom he introduced as his boss at the cable network, is going on and on about how this singer is destroying *the precious little that is left of American culture.* Mr. Greyhalle laughs, and the man seated next to him asks if American culture is really so fragile. The woman answers by saying, almost rudely, that it's *self-explanatory.*

The only self-explanatory thing about this singer is her ability to annoy. That's hardly enough power to destroy American culture.

And now everyone at the table is looking at me. I have, from some mixture of irritation and nerves, actually said this aloud. It would appear that I am the one who has spoken rudely. Oh, joy. I take a sip of water and try explaining.

"What I mean is, whenever I hear her, I think, *Please, God, no, don't let that song get stuck in my head.*"

"Leila's right," Eamon says. "The song does make you pray."

"Of course," the woman says. "And if I were as cute as Leila is, you'd agree with me."

"Elizabeth," Eamon says, his voice kinder than she deserves. "That's not true."

I keep in mind that this woman is his boss and that there's a limit to what he can say.

"What's true is you'll never be as cute," Brett says, in a clear attempt to lighten the charged, heavy air.

"Never be as young, you mean," Elizabeth says.

Underneath her words is the implication that there is something wrong with me for being young. And also something seriously wrong with Eamon for being in any way associated with me. In fact, Elizabeth has described me exactly the way she described the singer with the *ooohh ooohh* love song. She has dismissed us both as young and cute. It's hard not to think that this had been her intention from the start. Even before I said anything.

Isaac, with the ease of someone with years of experience in talking about himself, begins a long rambling speech about when he was young. Within minutes, I'm safely out of Elizabeth's firing range. I also have a splitting headache, and for the first time in my life pass up dessert.

Brett and one of the men switch places. He's the production designer Eamon thought I should meet. And he seems nice and interesting and I promise myself to rent DVDs of the movies he's mentioning, but right at this moment I couldn't care less about my future. I look around the table and catch Eamon looking at me. What am I doing here? What does he want?

It's in the cab ride home that I remember the only thing about today which has been important. What matters is not why Brett thinks Eamon cares where I go to college. Or why Elizabeth thinks I'm stupid but is only willing to say young and cute. It doesn't even matter that Isaac Rebinsehn is even more disappointing in person than in Charlotte's descriptions.

What matters about tonight is that Adrien Tilden wrote me. Although I do wonder about the wisdom of wanting to uncover my dead sister's secrets more than wanting to understand the people around me. Right now Eamon and his friends seems impossible to decipher. It's easier to focus on Rebecca.

I squash my doubts about the vague note from London and, as the city flashes by too quickly to see clearly, decide that by October I'll have answers.

Twenty-seven

I WAKE UP THE NEXT MORNING with red welts along the inside of my arms and at the base of my neck. They're a little itchy and I think maybe a spider has bitten me, but Clare takes one look and says,

"Stress hives. I used to get them all the time. I thought you said everything went well last night."

"It did," I say.

She finds some antihistamines in her briefcase and tells me to take a cold shower. And not to get too hot (good luck on the subway) or wear anything tight.

"Did you eat anything unusual last night?" she asks. "Shellfish? Strawberries?"

"No," I say. "It was lamb. With rice and salad."

"You'll be okay," she says, and kisses the top of my head before heading out for an early conference call.

Raphael gives me some money before he and I leave.

"Maybe take a cab today," he says.

The hives spread and grow into each other throughout the day. I feel like any second they'll spill out onto my hands and face. They itch like crazy. I don't remember what chickenpox was like, but this must be worse.

Eamon calls before taking his father out to the beach house for the weekend. He wants to apologize for Elizabeth.

"I know she was horrible," he says. "But she's a very useful person to know."

"Yes," I say. "She seemed it."

"Was Brett helpful at least?"

I look down at my arms, which are raging red. "I guess."

"I'll call you when I get back," he says. "Maybe we can go to Acca on Monday. I'll buy cake."

"Maybe," I say.

Charlotte sends me home early.

"It's making me itch to look at you," she says.

We don't go to the mountains and I spend most of the night sitting in cold bath water. Clare remembers that there was a cortisone-based cream that worked when she had hives and, on Saturday, tries to get hold of a doctor. But hers is out of town, as is my pediatrician.

"Dr. Shayle is a pediatrician?" Clare asks. "Do they think you're twelve?"

"I like him," I say. "It never hurts when he takes blood."

"Have you even been to the gynecologist?" Clare asks.

"Do we have to discuss this now?" I ask.

"Clare, it's hardly the pressing issue," Raphael says. "I'm going to call William."

Which is how I come to see him for the first time since Rebecca's service. He makes a house call because he doesn't want to prescribe cortisone over the phone. Clare and Raphael leave us alone as if I'm really having a doctor's appointment. Despite all my itching, I'm happy to see William and his beautiful small hands.

"You have a spectacular case of hives," he says after asking me an endless series of questions about my medical history. "It doesn't seem like it, I know, but the antihistamines are working."

"I look like Queen of the Rash," I say, suddenly feeling silly that we have summoned a surgeon for this.

William phones something into the pharmacy that will help dry out the welts. Raphael goes to pick it up, and before William leaves, Clare asks what he thinks about giving Rebecca's money to a Swedish university.

"She didn't have clear instructions," he says. "So she can hardly complain about her name winding up in a library. Or under a window. Do you, um, well, do you need any extra money?"

"No, no, no," Clare says. "No. I just wanted to check with the people who were important to her."

"Well, um, yes, well, thank you," William says. "Your father, though, I don't know that this, um, is an idea he'll love."

"I'm not asking him," Clare says. "Being in Poland means he gets to miss a whole lot of things."

So, she's mad at Da for being gone. I've wondered, although I'd believed her that she was fine with Da's going away. But how could she be? Her mother dies. A year later, her sister dies. And then her father asks for a huge favor before leaving her for a year. Of course she's mad. Not only at Da, but it's easier to be mad at him. Being mad at Rebecca is impossible.

"Yes, right, um, in Poland," William says. "I see. Listen, Leila, keep an eye on yourself. I don't think it's environmental, but stress-related. I'm not going to tell you to avoid stress, but don't overdo."

I'd like to hug him, but who'd want to touch me? However, he puts his arms around me, saying I'm not contagious. And to be good.

The cream does help, and Raphael drags his TV and DVD player into the room where I sleep. But, oddly, it's reading that takes my mind off my skin. I start on my ten pages of *Monte Cristo* and then go way past them. The main character did get out of prison and has been slowly planning his revenge on the people who put him there. He's been in Paris doing nothing but going to parties and then today, finally, he starts ruining the lives of the people who plotted to put him in prison. I read right through dinner—Clare brings me a tray—until I'm done.

Da was right. I really liked it. Okay, maybe not until the end, but that's a lot for me. And now that I know how it ends, I probably would like the rest of it more. I start all over and find it's much more fun when you can notice all the little details that are going to matter later.

I wonder at what point in the story this became a book Rebecca enjoyed. I suppose I could ask Clare, who may or may not know. But the bigger question is when will I get over wishing that I could ask things of my dead sister.

By Monday morning I look a lot better, but you can still see I had some kind of rash attack. Everyone at Charlotte's office says you can hardly see a thing, but I am not stupid. If you can hardly see something, it means the something is still there. When Eamon calls I wind up telling him the truth because I'm such a horrendous liar that he thinks I don't want to see him.

"I know Elizabeth was nasty," he says. "But did I do something?"

Well, yes. Your old girlfriend from years ago was acting like I'm next. So I'm guessing that's something you did or said.

"I have hives," I say, knowing I can never explain why Brett made me so uncomfortable. "I'd rather not see anyone."

"Hives? What are you allergic to?"

"Nothing," I say. "I just got lucky."

He laughs and says we'll have to make do with Wednesday.

It's when I'm finishing my cake that it occurs to me I am sitting smack in the middle of how I've pictured myself winding up. I'm in the café eating pastry; there's a book in my bag, and a man seated across from me at the table. Some of the details are wrong—the book isn't a difficult one that I understand, the table's not in the window, and Eamon is far too confusing to be my great love. However, I've pretty much decided that liking what

I read is more to the point than *conquering* it.

It seems to follow that if I can have that sort of freedom with books I'm certainly allowed to have it with the man who is, for one reason or another, here in my picture. I remember the question I thought of the other night: *What does he want from me?* I'm surprised at how little effort it takes. I don't feel either brave or nervous.

"Do you like me?" I ask. "I know that you don't and why you can't, but sometimes I think you do."

Eamon looks at me as if debating whether to say *That's not true* or *What are you talking about?*

I am tempted to add, for the sake of clarity, that I'm asking if he likes me as more than a friend, but the truth is if he pretends to misunderstand I'm going to get up from this table and walk away without ever regretting it.

"What do you want me to say?" he asks.

A question whose answer I've given no thought to whatsoever. Is it enough for him to say, *Yes, I like you.* Because then what? At some point he will leave the city and return to L.A. I may be ambitious, but at least five years stand between me and the start of any real work. I can see clearly how impossible this is.

And yet there's one question whose answer I have thought out, and it suddenly comes to mind. It's my useless question from months ago: What would I have told Rebecca if I'd known of her plan? My initial answers have given way to the one I hope I would have said, over and over. I know Eamon's question is different from the Rebecca one. But the answer is the same.

"Stay with me," I say, wishing I'd said it to my sister but also wanting to hear it from him.

"Stay with you?" he asks.

"No," I say. "You've messed up the pronoun."

It only takes him a minute to see what I mean.

"Leila, you're not wrong to think that I like you," he says. "And if things were different, I would say exactly that."

"I have to be twenty," I say.

"No . . . it's not . . . no," he says.

"Smarter?"

"No," he says. "God, no."

I look down at my plate, happy enough to see that there's some cake left.

"It's just all wrong," he says. "You're starting out and I'm well past that."

"But you like me anyway," I say, so as to be clear.

"Yes," he says. "I thought it would be enough for us to ignore that."

"It should be," I say. "But, you know, I get mixed up easily. And I have a boyfriend I've been mean to."

I could also tell him about when Rebecca died. How everyone I knew got wrapped up in her being gone; my father took my mother with him and Clare's and Raphael's every move was shaped by my sister's death. And how he fits into all of this by making me feel protected from the ultimate *poof, vanished*. But I don't say anything because this is rapidly becoming one of those times when words don't work.

"Mean how?" Eamon asks, and I have to think to understand what he's saying. Ben. He wants to know about Ben.

"Oh, well, I stopped sleeping with him," I say. "And then wouldn't start. Start it again."

Eamon tries not to laugh, which I don't appreciate, and a small smile escapes him.

"I don't think that's considered mean by most people," Eamon says. "It's one of those things that happens. He'll get over it."

I'll wipe that smug look clear.

"Except I wouldn't sleep with him again because I wanted to with you," I say.

He doesn't say anything, but he is also no longer smiling.

It's clear we can't sit here forever. Surely there's nothing left to say about what is both *impossible* and *all wrong*. I'm the one forcing the issue, so I should probably be the one to leave. On the other hand, this is more my café than his. Once he's gone, I'll still have a book in my bag and cake to eat. This is *my* picture of how I've ended up so far.

"I think I can only afford to be confused by Rebecca right now," I say. "And I can't change being seventeen."

"I know," he says.

You know. Well, this is it.

"I'm going to close my eyes," I say. "And when I open them, you'll be gone, and maybe when I'm done starting out, I'll come to California and find you."

"Leila," he says.

"We'll go from there," I say, amazed at how incredibly sad this makes me. And relieved.

He's quiet for a while, saying, finally, "You have this spot on your neck."

My hands fly up to my collarbones, where the worst of my hives had appeared. I thought they were all gone and simply cannot believe they've shown up again.

"No, not that," he says, his hand reaching for my neck, wrapping around it until his fingertips settle into the long, narrow groove in the back. "This."

The warmth and pressure of his hand spread and travel through me.

"If you let me stay," he says, "we could take it from here."

It is both quick and slow, lingering in certain places while not quite vanishing in others.

I nod. Yes. Okay.

"I inexcusably adore you," he says.

The sad feeling has disappeared, but also the relief.

"It will go all wrong," he says.

Only the yes remains.

"Inevitably," he says.

"Thanks for the sales pitch," I say, but cover his hand with mine.

Twenty-eight

I WALK HOME WITH MY NECK aflame and my body pleasantly heavy, knowing I have to do what I should have done months ago. I think of a carefully worded, brilliant e-mail and then remember I'll have to write it. So instead I go to Clare. For the kind of help I could never have gotten from Rebecca.

"Do I need to call Elsa?" Clare asks when I have spelled everything out for her. "Are they going to feel like I failed them if I don't send you off to a Swiss convent school?"

"No," I say.

"If Raphael didn't like Eamon so much, it's what he'd do."

"Mom thinks I should be true to what I want," I say. "And I'm not asking for a permission slip. It's about writing to Ben."

"Use the telephone," Clare says. "If you break up with him via e-mail, you'll never forgive yourself."

The call, which I dread, goes less than well. I say, as clearly and easily as possible, that I want to go out with someone from work. That I almost wish I didn't, but that Ben deserves someone not interested in anyone but him. He wants to know what school Eamon goes to and I say, *He's older.*

"What do you mean, 'older'?" Ben asks. "We'll be seniors. He's in college?"

"He's thirty-one," I say. "He writes for television."

Silence.

"You realize there's only one thing he wants from you," Ben says finally. "I mean, Leila, really. It can't be your brains he's after. It's not like you're at all smart."

I've hurt his feelings by not wanting him the way he wanted me. And the price for this is to be called stupid.

"I'm so sorry," I say. "You were my—"

But he hangs up before I can finish. Which, in a way, saves me from having to regret whatever useless words I had in mind.

Raphael goes to Ben's apartment to get My Scott,

who's then sent to live with Clare's boss, Edward. Who assures me he's a cat lover from way back and is glad to be able to do us a favor.

Eamon and I go out to dinner, as first suggested in May. Kissing is no longer a one-time event, but it's still the way I remember it. I worried it would be like an éclair, which is always a better idea than an actual dessert. Being with him is pretty much what it's always been, but without the keeping secret how much I *want* to be with him.

He comes with me to see plays. Charlotte has been offering me free tickets all summer. Both Clare and Raphael work late more often than not, so I've only gone a few times by myself. A lot of the fun is discussing it afterward, which is probably why I've always liked reading plays more than books. They're for a group audience, which makes it less lonely.

"It's the same in TV," Eamon says one night. "Film, too. Except that those group audiences are unbelievably huge compared to theater."

I think of the DVDs I promised myself to rent when I spoke to the production designer at Mr. Greyhalle's apartment. And of Brett's comments about the director in Texas going past schedule and overbudget. The part of Charlotte's job that I like the most is the work before the play happens. If Brett is right and the invisible work for a movie is *immense,* then maybe I would like it.

"Can we watch movies where you know the people who did the work?" I ask Eamon. "Or TV shows?"

"Of course," he says. "Do you have any in mind?"

"Well, I want to know more about what kind of work makes a movie possible," I say.

"I can get you on a set," he says. "Maybe not here, but definitely in L.A."

"Are you asking me to go to California?" I ask him, thinking of Brett again.

"I'm not," he says.

"You don't want me to go to school there?"

"Leila, be fair," he says. "I cannot ask my seventeen-year-old girlfriend to plan her future on anything having to do with me."

This makes a kind of sense. I'm likely to change my mind about lots of things, and I won't thank him if I make decisions because of what he wants.

"However, should you find yourself in California," he says, "I can arrange a set visit. I don't even have to be in town to do that."

"Let's start by looking at some of your shows," I say.

"Repeats or anything where you know what the work was like."

"Okay," he says. "That I can also do."

Both movies and television, I decide, are much more interesting if you either know or are trying to figure out how and why certain things were done. Not just stunts, but casting, locations, and, in TV at least, ridiculous plot twists.

After seeing a loud and badly staged musical that I can't believe is still running, Eamon and I go to a small Spanish restaurant on Sixteenth Street. It's full of square tables, red candles, and an onion smell. After we both agree that it takes a lot more than one great tap dancer to make a musical work, a silence settles over us. The same uneasy kind I remember from the first time Ben and I went out, as if the word *date* had taken away our ability to talk.

I scan the menu as I always do, looking for the cheapest item so as to eliminate it from my order. I've somehow managed to make Janie's rules keep me company. If they're ridiculous, they're also things I know. I look over at Eamon, who is still shrouded in quiet.

I tap on his wineglass. "What is it?"

Which is when he tells me that the person he's been subletting his New York apartment to is moving out.

"I've decided not to renew the sublease," he says. "It looks like my show's going to get picked up, and even if Dad agrees to some live-in help, I should stay and keep an eye on him. For a bit."

We've both been pretending we aren't waiting for exactly this. In spite of my pointing out that I've only ever had sex in a "parental" apartment, Eamon has said he isn't prepared to bring me to his father's for anything beyond my company.

"There's an advantage to not being seventeen," he told me. "You still think about it all the time, but you're more in control of your actions."

And you have your own apartment. Which is about to be empty.

"So," I say.

"So," he says.

Thundering silence. And, then.

"Before we find ourselves there," he says. "If we find ourselves there," he adds. "Is there anything you want to ask me?"

"Um, no," I say. "Should there be?"

"Well, yes," he says, but doesn't elaborate.

"Oh, I know, what's written on your ring?" I ask, sure this isn't what he means, but still curious.

He takes the ring off and hands it to me, saying, "It's supposedly Tibetan about how everything changes and that our bodies are an illusion, but for all I know it's gibberish."

I look at it, running my finger over the symbols as if they were Braille. Gibberish or no, it makes me think of this one special class we had during tenth grade. It was run by our biology teacher and she started it by talking on and on about how our bodies change and our needs and how to inform ourselves.

"I know what you want me to ask," I say to him. "It's about AIDS."

"That's how it starts," Eamon says.

I wait. He can consider himself asked.

He's not had an AIDS test for three years, he tells me, and I can certainly ask him to.

"You should, in fact, always ask," he says. "If nothing else, it gives you a stalling technique."

"A stalling technique for what?"

"You know, if you want to wait," he says.

"Oh, God, this again," I say. "You want to wait until I'm twenty?"

"Leila, no, not quite," he says. "Not really at all,

although, well, of course we can."

He doesn't sound very convinced, which I think is worth noticing.

"We'll wait until we know we want to," he says, adding with a laugh, "until you know. I obviously know."

"I've wanted to since we shook hands at Acca," I say, wondering if he really thinks I don't already know. "I was all, *wow*."

One look at his face—startled and slightly embarrassed—tells me that this is the sort of information one keeps to oneself. It could be worse. I could have told him that my body is the one thing in life which I completely trust.

It breaks out in hives when unhappy. It demands that I eat food I love on a daily basis. In spite of the needing a bra issue, it looks nice in certain clothes. My body's beating heart and coiled bliss were what told me that being in a dark theater was the closest I would get to heaven. The chronic headache that faded after months with my tutor let me know I might find a way to be dyslexic and live. Out here in the world.

My body gets up every day and falls asleep when it's had it. It's my best self and mine to keep or share. Waiting won't change that.

"You were all, *wow?*" Eamon asks, looking a bit recovered.

"I think the words I used were zing-zang-zoom," I say, and we are back to flirting, which is nice, as I hadn't known you could do that with your boyfriend.

"My words were please, please help me find a way to ask this girl out," he says. "And all I had to do was read a book."

Right, of course. He read that book so he could date me. It wasn't to be nice or because he was interested. I totally missed that. I wonder what else he's done with a motive I didn't see.

I was badly prepared by that biology class. In theory, it sounded easy. And this is fairly easy because it's with Eamon. But what if it was with someone you didn't know as well? Is that the point? That you only sleep with someone you can have the talk with? That seems reasonable, but only in theory.

"Does everyone have this conversation before?" I ask. "About waiting and stuff?"

For once I'm glad that I don't have the right words, because other than AIDS I'm not sure what I mean by *stuff*.

"It's supposed to happen naturally," Eamon says.

Ben insisted on talking about it months before we

needed to because his brother told him that if I got pregnant, his life would be over. He made me feel like I was putting him in danger. And then, when it was time, I was the one who had to say, *Wait*.

"It's a talk women usually start," Eamon says. "Which explains why I'm doing it badly."

I think of the things I've learned by accident—when to accept jewelry and what to order—and know I'm glad to be learning how to negotiate the where, the when, and the importance of sex.

"You're doing fine," I say.

"Good, thanks," he says. "So are you."

"Will we be graded?" I ask.

"We'll be judged," he says. "That'll be enough."

Clare gives me a new set of rules. I cannot spend the night with him. I need to check in with her more often about where I am. The minute I look unhappy or if, once school starts again, my grades slip, this is over. Also, I do realize, right, that it's not going to last forever. Not because Eamon is a bad person, but that without *a certain commonality* that being *roughly* the same age provides, *the odds are against it*.

"I'm not thinking about forever," I tell her. "It's okay to plan for now, right?"

"Of course," Clare says. "And you know, it says a lot of good things about him that he likes you. I just want you to be prepared."

"I have college and work and all of that to prepare for, to last forever," I say.

When it ends, as he says it inevitably will, or if it ends, which is how I prefer to think of it, preparing won't help me.

"Just don't get hurt," she says.

"Not on your watch, huh," I say.

"No, I mean not ever," Clare says. "Love's hard. Be careful."

I hug her because even if I can't follow the advice, it's a long way from the elegant kindness which used to be the only thing she gave me.

I don't know if this counts as preparing, but I find myself forming a new picture of how I'll wind up. No sitting in a café and no eating cake this time, although there are books, but only ones I love. In this new end of my particular story, I have an apartment. It has plants, a well-stocked kitchen, photos of the lost hotels, and a cat. From this place, I go to work, although I can't see yet if it's for movies, TV, or theater. While in the apartment, I conduct my life without grades, judgments, or warnings.

Twenty-nine

EAMON'S BODY HAS A TEXTURE and a quality that is different from any I would have imagined, if I had thought to imagine such a thing. And then, for rather a while, I don't think. Things happen which I had not thought could occur with someone else in the room. It's as if he has been practicing on my body for as long as I have.

When my thoughts finally return, they are of the churches in Poland, with their great, open spaces reserved for those who want a sacred quiet. Of the care taken in everything from the benches to the altar. The oddness and beauty of a hush that almost lets you hear your own blood.

"A cathedral?" Eamon asks.

He is by the end of my description getting me some ice water. I now understand how you know when you want to and with whom. It must be this lack of doubt that's making me think of church.

"Yes," I say, still on the bed.

I can't quite believe all the different ways my body is soaring and humming. In a second I will put on my shirt and underwear and go stand in front of the air conditioner.

"I don't think I've ever been told that," he says, bringing the water and my clothes back to the bed. "Here, let me."

No one has helped me into my clothes with this level of gentle attention since I was five.

"What did they tell you?" I ask him.

He kisses my shoulder. "Church is great, it's definitely the best."

There's such a gap between the images I carry in my mind and what can actually be found in the world. Which is why it takes a few visits for me to see how similar Eamon's apartment is to the one I've been imagining. It's smaller and in a less good neighborhood, but it's clean, full of books and has French movie posters hanging on the walls. In the kitchen, he keeps bottles of water, tuna salad with olives, and plastic containers of sliced cantaloupe, which I eat with my fingers.

"Do you speak French?" I ask, thinking of Paris, where the Abranels first lived after leaving Egypt.

"I've no second language at all," Eamon says. "Mostly this was a cheap and easy way to decorate."

The place in L.A. is nicer, he says. Less crowded, more sun, better view. The reason he keeps this apartment is because while no one would ever choose to live so close to Avenue D, he can't bring himself to let go of the lease. The rent's very low, although more than it was eight years ago when he first moved in.

"You didn't go to L.A. right after school?"

"My first job was running errands for the writing staff on a soap opera," Eamon says. "It was worse than the job you already have for Charlotte. At least you get to answer the phone."

For the soap opera, he researched fatal illnesses, amnesia, adoption laws, and prenuptial agreements. At night, he wrote spec scripts for his favorite shows and sent them out until he got a real job. It sounds like a great time.

"Why television?" I ask.

A direct question about work. Old habits are often the best ones.

"I'm good at it," Eamon says. "I understand what works and what doesn't."

"You didn't want to write short stories?" I ask, thinking of the Fitzgerald stories full of rich and beautiful people losing their precious blonde girls.

It occurs to me that they were the first things I enjoyed reading and that I probably panicked at the novel because my tutor wouldn't shut up about how I wasn't reading *properly*. There were things in *Tender Is the Night* that I did like without understanding fully. Next time, I'm going to like what I like and let understanding fall where it may.

"No short stories," he says, arranging tuna on a cracker and offering it to me. "I do what I do."

"It is what it is," I say.

Of course Rebecca would be here. In some ways, I have him because I lost her. Best not to think about, I know, but hard to ignore.

"That's a little embittered for my taste," he says. "It's more I do what I do because I'm lucky and I like it."

Even if I didn't already have other reasons to like him—to love him, which I have managed to do in spite of its being an *all wrong* relationship—this particular statement would seal the deal.

What's left of the summer melts away so easily that even Rebecca's birthday feels like a bump sailed over instead of a mountain with frightening proportions. The last long weekend at the beginning of September brings the start-over feeling that always comes with packs of paper and three-ring binders. Although school is not where I shine, I like the little rituals it involves. New shoes, sensible skirts, cotton sweaters, and a class schedule.

On walls which are the same but different, posters announce auditions, meetings, practice schedules, and sign-ups for things like the debate team. Ben likes to say that debates are where our school allows the closest thing to fistfights. *Liked* to say it, that is. Once upon a time he said it to me.

Apparently our spat on the phone was not enough. I have, thanks to my best friend and former boyfriend, become a rumor at school. Girls I barely know now approach me as if we've been in the habit of keeping each other updated about all that is important. From things they say about their own experiences with men, dating, and sex, I can tell they think they know something about me. Something which is probably not quite true.

I set out to discover what kind of information Ben has released into the school. He's done it rather well, and if it weren't about me I'd admire the method. It took a few well-chosen words to younger boys with sisters in my grade. It's the boys themselves who bring me up to date. They're the ones from seventh grade who think I'm so fun to look at.

And are now in the eighth grade, which they quickly point out before passing on what they know. I'm the new It Girl of Trash, they tell me, having practically forced myself on Ben only to move on to an *old guy*. Anyone who has met my *elderly* father knows I have issues no *normal guy* could resolve. I'll always want, they tell me, a boyfriend old enough to be my father.

Okay, this is so beyond yuck. It's just nasty enough to make me want a shower. There's no point screaming that Eamon is only fourteen years older than I am. And therefore *not* old enough to be my father. Gross.

"Is your dad really like, you know, your grandfather?" one of the boys asks me.

"No," I say, thinking of *Chinatown*, which Eamon and I watched the other night because this was *a classic I had to see*. "He's my father and my brother."

Draw a family chart explaining *that*. I'm overly pleased to have stunned them into speechlessness.

I decide to make myself too busy to dwell on the

implications of what Ben has chosen to stress and immediately find that I'm busy without any effort. For the first time ever, I'm genuinely caught up in my classes. Raphael is thrilled to be helping with precalculus, and I start to see how shapes really do come out of those equations. They're totally connected, the way measurements and building plans are. In English we're finally reading the Chekhov plays, which gives me a chance to test my theory about rereading being more fun than it sounds. School is still hard, but I'm not navigating the fog so much as watching it part.

And, then, almost without warning, the anniversary of the attack on the city is upon us. Raphael decides to go to a church service being offered at St. Patrick's. He says that a lot of the people who died probably did believe in God, so who is he to be an atheist? This was their home too.

Clare doesn't think the cathedral is *her* home, exactly, and asks if she can walk me to school. I suspect that it's one morning she doesn't want to be alone in the office. We both stop on the sidewalk at exactly eight forty-six for the minute of silence, even though no one else does. I remember how much I wanted my mother that day. How I watched the news without moving but that it didn't sink in until that night.

Although we didn't know it then, more bad news was on the way. What did Rebecca think? I suppose she could have thought it was a good time to be leaving. After all, what a mess, but wasn't she curious to know how it would end? Especially with the *it* so big and impossible. I hug Clare before turning toward school.

"I could kill her for not being here," my sister says.

Well, yes. I suppose.

"And I miss Gyula," she says. "Still. I can't stop myself."

My hearts cracks a little for Raphael. Although if I love Eamon partly because of Rebecca, then it's only fair to see how my cousin has Clare for the exact same reason.

"You're allowed to miss him," I say.

Maybe great love is simply the love that fits. That would explain what happened to Julian and Janie. It wasn't ruined because it ended. It ended when they no longer fit each other. Da and my mother fit and so do Clare and Raphael. Gyula did fit with Clare once, but the shape of her life changed after Rebecca died.

"I'm not allowed to, actually," Clare says. "And I shouldn't."

Even I know that *should* rarely carries the day for this kind of thing.

"Gyula still thinks you have a date in November," I say. "You could call him."

"We'll see," Clare says. "Not a day for acting on how you feel."

I'm late for the memorial assembly because I stay outside to watch my fiercely beautiful sister walk off into her life of hotels, contracts, and decisions. I know that at some point she will find a way to handle it. I also know I would do anything—even get on a plane—to keep her from being hideously unhappy. So would Raphael and maybe even Gyula, if he knew how close he's come to forever blowing it.

Thirty

AS A SENIOR THIS YEAR, I can design an independent study to be overseen by Mr. Nordman, our headmaster. I remember when I first heard about this option (from Ben, of course, who is going to build a computer) I thought, *No thanks.* But over the summer, one of the people I met through Charlotte thought that I should consider reading and studying *some plays from antiquity.* The recommendations were *Medea, Antigone,* and *Oedipus Rex,* and the idea was that if I could come up with set designs for these plays, I could come up with anything.

Of the three plays, only *Antigone* appealed to me. The first line is *O Sister . . . dear, dear sister.* Antigone kills herself after being sentenced to death for trying to bury her brother's body. Her boyfriend and then his mother kill themselves from grief. At first I thought I liked the play because here were three suicides you could understand. You could even, given the way the play is written, support them.

But it was mostly that I had a great design idea for the tower and the battlefield, which I gave to Raphael for approval and then to Eamon for showing off. He thought I might want to read *Mourning Becomes Electra*.

"It's kind of based on *Antigone*," he said. "And it's the same guy who wrote *Ah, Wilderness*, which you've been carrying around all summer."

It's also endless (three plays in one) and, as plays go, not the easiest read in the world. As a result, it takes me longer than it should to put a proposal together. I make an appointment to see Mr. Nordman in his office, which smells slightly musty, in order to ask for an extension.

"You want to do an independent study?" he asks, sounding shocked. "Are you sure?"

"I think so," I say, wondering if I'm doomed to travel through life always considered some variation of less than bright.

What did Janie say? That my skin would go to hell and people would think I was stupid. Why didn't I ask her more about that?

"The deadline's next Friday. I'll give you an extra week," Mr. Nordman says. "Until October eleventh."

"Thanks," I say. "That's great."

"Leila, that'll be the Friday before Columbus Day," he says. "If you miss it, I can't make an exception."

I have a calendar. I know when the eleventh is. Rehearsals for *Ah, Wilderness* start on the following Tuesday, which is the fifteenth. The calendar is something I've never had trouble reading. I smile brightly over my wanting to smack him.

"Thank you."

Clare gives me a cell phone. It's on her account and she'll pay for it, within reason. We're having one of our home-alone nights even though it's not Thursday. She says Raphael has some things to do at home and that she's too tired to go to German class. We eat dinner and I spread my homework out across the floor. Eamon calls at around ten and we take our usual twenty minutes to say nothing more than hi, I'm thinking of you and I'll call again soon. We have this conversation at least twice a day, even on days we've seen each other.

Tonight I tell him I have a new phone and give him the number.

He writes it down, asking, "What did she do that for?"

"I don't know," I say. "Maybe she thinks I'll need one in California."

I like to tease him about this. He has such a heart attack at the idea of people thinking I will go where he wants me to. It's funny that he thinks I'll get into a specific college just because I want to.

"Good night, bunny," he says. "I'll talk to you soon."

"Night," I say, thinking that *soon* is my favorite word.

"I have meetings in Vienna at the end of next week," Clare says when I sit back down on the floor.

"Okay," I say.

"It means I won't be here when you meet with Mr. Nordman," she says. "I'm sorry."

"I'll be fine," I say. "You have to work."

"I might see Gyula," she says.

I'm not surprised. Or sad or pleased by this news. I don't think I'll be anything until I know how she is.

"You called him," I say.

"No, I haven't decided yet," she says. "If there's time and I want to, I'll take the early train to Budapest. Meet him for lunch."

"Raphael doesn't know," I say.

"There's nothing to know," she says. "I don't even know."

I think of saying that he won't mind, she needn't worry. But something in Clare's face—a combination of exhaustion and misery—reminds me of what she said during one of her weepy nights after the breakup.

"It's Rebecca," I say. "You need to find out if you left Gyula because of Rebecca."

"I just wish I knew if I love Raphael or miss her," Clare says.

"Both, maybe?"

"Yes, but . . ." she says, trailing off. "God, the thing I'll never forgive her for is how many of my thoughts start that way now."

I suppose that's why I want there to be *a* reason. So I can forgive her.

Wait, I think. Wait. How did we move from Clare to Rebecca. That's not good.

"When you see Gyula," I say, "you'll know. And then you'll do the right thing."

"I hope I'll know what the right thing is," Clare says.

I move my books to the coffee table and get a sheet out of the cabinet I made for her birthday.

"Is he your great love?" I ask, taking cushions from the couch. "Gyula, I mean."

Clare is quiet for a little bit, watching me make up her bed.

"I could tell you I don't believe in them," she says.

"You could," I say.

"Maybe it's all a question of timing and there's no one person."

If that were true, Raphael would be winning the timing contest and she would not be sitting here planning to see Gyula.

"I think Mama and Da had a great love," Clare says. "But what a mess."

"Me too," I say, unreasonably thrilled to find another believer in my favorite Abranel story. "I've always thought that too. And the mess doesn't change it."

The mess is the most important part, as it sent him off to fall in love with my mother. Which is, after all, how I am here.

"You know, before Rebecca died, I'd never have left him," Clare says. "Not even if he'd bought me six hotels. I'd have just laughed and told him no."

"So he is your great love," I say. "Or was."

Or would have been. It makes sense that the man who reminds me of a chandelier is going to beat out the man who reminds me of my family. But being the great love doesn't mean being the love who lasts. Da and Janie have shown me that. Raphael would happily take being the one who lasts. Only Clare can decide.

"Do you want me to come with you?" I ask. "To Vienna, I mean."

"Oh, no, sweetie," she says. "I'll be fine."

"I can ask for another extension," I say, not caring that I won't get it. "When you come back from Budapest, you shouldn't be alone."

"Listen, when I take you to Europe," she says, "it will be on a trip just for us. We'll eat sweets and look at old buildings until our eyes fall out."

I picture us in Sweden, visiting the university's library with our sister's name in it. In Vienna or Munich, checking up on Clare's work projects. Or in Barcelona, staying at the Vivfilli. We might go to Alexandria together and hunt for Da's lost city. I can even see us trying to find a city with no stories in it at all. If we're lucky we'll have time for each possible trip.

Thirty-one

OCTOBER ARRIVES. From the moment I received Adrien Tilden's letter, I had imagined that this month would find me counting down the days until his return from London. Instead, two days go by before I think of my tentatively scheduled date to meet him. And then I only remember it because he sends me another note.

Dear Leila, My return home has been unexpectedly delayed. Scott and I will remain in London until December, possibly February. I hope we can meet then and talk about your sister. I have, of course, endlessly reviewed my last meeting with R. Obviously, I wish I'd known it would be the last, for it was just a quick cup of coffee to catch up on trivial news. I remember telling Scott that she looked beautiful and for that I am grateful. My best to you and your family. Cordially, Adrien.

I touch where he has written *R*. I want more than

anything to believe that his abbreviation of my sister's name is proof that he knew her in some special way. And that what he thinks is trivial might be something else entirely. I suppose that Scott might be Adrien's boyfriend (maybe even the man I saw him with at Acca), but who knows. If Adrien were gay, would that tell me more or less about Rebecca?

December, I think. I'll know in December. Or February. What exactly I'll know seems as vague as my new deadline. I tuck the note away with the first one and then find that I hardly think of it.

It must be that my thoughts are mostly taken up with worrying about Clare's upcoming trip to see Gyula. And with Eamon's inviting me to his father's beach house for the first weekend of the month.

Raphael says I can go, but Clare says I have to call my parents to ask.

"Mom already knows we're dating," I say.

I loved how she paused slightly before saying, *Yes, I thought that might happen.* From across the ocean and over the phone, I could feel her belief in my ability to know what was right. We stayed on the phone for another half-hour discussing obvious details, but nothing was as important as her initial response.

"I know she does," Clare says. "But a weekend trip

is something I want them to sign off on."

Da answers. Mom's out; she stayed late at the hospital. Instead of leaving a message for her to call, I decide to ask him.

"Clare hasn't said no, has she?" he asks.

"She says I need your permission."

"Those days are rapidly ending," Da says. "I gather you like this boy."

"He's thirty-one," I say. "And I do."

"Go with Eamon, have a good time," Da says. "Someday you'll tell me all about it."

I see that when she died, the gaping hole Rebecca made in Da's life was one that reached into his future. Whatever plans he'd once had included all of us telling him some version of how we were. Of what our lives were like.

"Someday," I say. "I promise."

It's a really nice weekend. Mr. Greyhalle tells me that even if I'm young enough to be doing homework, I have to call him Theodore. That he went to Stanford and can tell me that California is a great place to live.

"Dad," Eamon says. "Don't."

I spend most of my time in the small room Eamon

has taken over for his computer and scripts. Its sparseness—table, chair, shelves, one lamp—and its view of the ocean make it soothing and disturbing all at once. The way I have seen work itself to be.

Once back home, I finally tell Eamon what is being said about me at school. It's the night before my proposal is due, and I'm practicing the presentation. Apparently, I also find it easier to talk about myself if it's buried in and around work. Schoolwork, in this case, but that's what I have. I somewhat haltingly get out that people seem to think there's something deeply wrong with me. Wrong because of Da's age.

"They're really scraping for dirt," Eamon says. "It's been that bad?"

"Well, the girls all think I'm incredibly cool," I say.

"Cool doesn't sound so awful," he says. "Boys the ones giving you a problem?"

"Other than Ben, not the ones my age," I say. "But the theory about Da is floating around."

"And you're hearing it," he says, putting his arms around me.

"Yeah, you could say that."

I lean against him so his body can do that trick where it absorbs all the bad stuff.

"It's kind of playing out the opposite for me," he says. "The men all think I've done something brilliant and, except for Brett, the women think I should be shot."

I laugh because of the image he presents. A bunch of men sitting around thinking, *Hey, way to go, a blonde teenager,* and a bunch of women thinking that Eamon is also thinking that.

"Only my father is not being a jerk," Eamon says. "Who knew."

"And Brett."

"Brett always thinks the best of me," he says. "She knows I did not run after you hoping you didn't know any better."

She may have made me uneasy, but I'll probably have to wind up liking her. I'll just have to stay away from Elizabeth.

"Is that what people are saying to you?" I ask. "That I don't know better?"

"That's the nice version," he says. "Listen, bunny, look at me."

I retreat to the end of the couch in his father's living room. We spend a fair amount of time at Mr. Greyhalle's apartment, which radically cuts down on how often we sleep together. I think I know now why we're here so much instead of at Eamon's. It's not just because he's worried about his dad. Eamon's as afraid as I am that what we're hearing might be true.

Maybe I should tell him that calling me *bunny* isn't helping what people say, but I like it. I'd be sorry if I never heard him say it again. I can live with a little speculation.

"There's no way people aren't going to have an opinion about us," he says. "It's annoying, I know."

"It's creepy and weird."

"That's actually a better description," he says and then adds, in a TV announcer voice, "Leila and Eamon, the creepy and the weird: tune in Tuesdays at eight."

"But you don't write sitcoms," I say.

"I think I get to be the monster in this one," he says. "Not the writer."

"Let's make it animation," I say, because it killed him to lose the details in the Japanese animated version. He said even a genius couldn't make up for it.

"If we were a show, we'd already have broken up," Eamon says. "It's bad for ratings if a couple stays together."

"According to you, we're going to break up," I say, but I can't look at him, and fix my eyes on the rug. "Even Clare thinks it can't last, and she likes you."

"Leila, what if we agree to let people think what they want," he says. "And to not care as long as we don't feel creepy and weird."

"Why would we?" I ask, looking up, because in all my life I've never felt as right and as certain as when I'm with him.

"Sometimes it's easier to believe other people instead of listening to what you hope for," he says.

"Did you hope for this?" I ask, motioning to the space between us as if we were connected by the air.

"Only secretly," he says. "I was afraid it would feel too strange."

"But it doesn't," I say.

"I know," he says. "I was wrong."

Which means it's possible his belief about what will *inevitably* go all wrong is just that—a belief. Inexcusable adoration, which has made me feel absurdly happy as well as protected, might well go in any number of directions.

Eamon could be nothing but the beginning of all the misery and heartbreak ahead as I look for a love to fit with my life in the theater. Or, I could find myself at a dinner party someday, warning another girl that he can still make me do anything. There may even be an end we have neither heard of nor thought to imagine.

Mr. Nordman asks several questions during my presentation, mostly having to do with the designs instead of the plays. It's a good thing I made some sketches instead of only relying on dimensions and scale. When I'm done he says it's the best independent study proposal he's ever approved.

"Good for you, Leila," he says. "I was so pleased when your grades picked up last year."

"Why?" I ask.

Everyone cares so much about my grades. Surely I'm more than the arrangement of letters I get in exchange for studying.

"Because you're very bright," he says, words I never hoped to hear from a non–family member. "I've always thought it."

That's not true. He's not always thought any such thing.

"How could you possibly ever think that?" I ask him. "I take all my tests untimed, reading a math problem takes almost as long as answering it. I'm not bright, I'm a struggle."

I sound angry, which isn't right since he's giving me a compliment.

"But you haven't given up," Mr. Nordman says. "In my book, that's bright."

"Yes, well, um," I say, my mind going blindingly blank. "So I need to, um, hand in my first draft by, uh . . . when?"

Could I sound more like William when he's nervous? What's wrong with me?

"Let's say end of January, with check-ins on your progress twice a month," Mr. Nordman says. "That way you can focus on exams and college applications."

"Right, okay," I say. "Thanks."

I gather up my designs, note cards, and books and bolt out of his office as if it's on fire. Something's wrong, out of place, not in order. Through my last two periods I scan my mind over and over. What is it? The proposal? No, it's not school.

Eamon asked me to call him and tell him how it went. If I felt like celebrating, I could meet him at Acca. If I didn't feel like it, I could meet him there anyway. I could use my new cell or the pay phone on the corner, but I walk right by it and go home.

It's only once there, when I head straight into my closet, that I know what's wrong. I slip the ring Da gave me on New Year's Day off its ribbon and put it on my right middle finger. If I want to, I can drop knitting from the antidyslexic schedule. I now have a guarantee that I'll keep left straight from right.

This ring was my sister's, and if once I wished she'd given it to me, I'll wear it forever precisely because she didn't. I don't need a sign or a clue or even a meeting with Adrien Tilden to find out the reason for what happened.

Rebecca gave up.

Which is unbelievably sad and totally inexcusable.

For a minute I think I'm going to have the kind of crying fit that demands running water and a closed door. But instead I sit quietly, waiting as things shift and crack. It is exactly as Clare described them doing for her on that trip to Sweden when she was first able to notice cups, flowers, soap. When she could see what was there.

Adrien Tilden turned out to be a real person, but I made him more important than what he actually is— someone left behind. I hunted for Rebecca's hidden story and wished for a secret reason because I couldn't bear to think about what she had done.

Eventually, I go into the bathroom and hold my hand up to the mirror. I'll be glad to meet Adrien, the way I'll always be glad to touch or remember even the smallest part of her life. From a box under my bed, I pull out the picture of Da, Janie, and Clare. The one

Rebecca took of them on her birthday. I snuck it out of my father's study and packed it with my things when I left to come here.

It's probably the best photograph I have of her, reflecting as it does the way I knew her best, through stories involving other people.

When Janie died, people told Da and the girls to, somehow, *get through a year*. Eventually, *time would heal all wounds*. That's all Gyula meant when he told Clare to wait before she left him, but I don't think a year is going to heal her. Or Da. Or even me.

There's no end to the kind of angry that Rebecca's giving up demands. Instead it leaks out here and there, both hideous and pretty. Things turn out differently than they might have.

There's no story in it. No narrative waiting to be put into its proper sequence. So I'll stop looking before the year is up. After all, when I tell myself the story of Rebecca's suicide, I start with meeting Janie, which took place years before. At some point, this story might become one about how I met Eamon. Or Charlotte. Depending on who is more important by the time I get to that apartment I've imagined.

Clare's Rebecca story will always be part of how she chose either her great love or her cousin. Da's will involve, rather cleverly, helping to create a hospital.

Rebecca erased a part of each of us. It's how we fill it back in that will be what survives. What is told.

Acknowledgments

It is customary, as my father would say, to thank people and to cite the books on which the writer has relied.

Therefore, I shall start with Thomas Weyr. It is from him that I have learned exactly what it means to be the daughter of a man who has lost his city. His book, *The Setting of the Pearl: Vienna Under Hitler*, will give some idea of what I owe him. He gave me invaluable editing suggestions at different times.

For Clare's and Leila's vague ideas and dreams about Alexandria, *False Papers* by André Aciman and *A Blood-Dimmed Tide* by Amos Elon were very helpful in quite different ways.

For Clare's career—and love—of hotels, I am indebted to my mother. From the time I was very small, she took me with her on both personal and business trips throughout Europe. The hotels were almost always for budget-minded businesspeople or local tourists. As such, they were full of stories and she allowed me to roam through them freely. She also gave me *New Hotels for Global Nomads* by Donald Albrecht to help in my research.

The following people gave generously of their time and attention as readers: Elizabeth Thompson, Katie Smythe-Newman, Rosina Williams, Mathew Olshan, Aliyah Baruchin, and my sainted agent, Robin Rue. My editor, Margaret Raymo, had questions and comments which were most illuminating. My husband, Jeffrey Freymann-Weyr, read each and every draft with unfailing patience. His clarity and wisdom are of incalculable help.